WE ARE ALL
HIS CREATURES

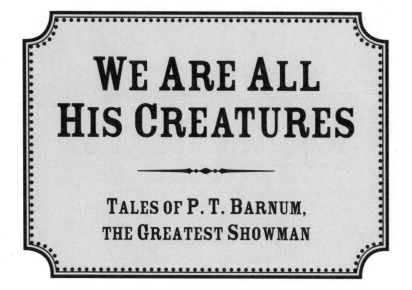

WE ARE ALL HIS CREATURES

TALES OF P. T. BARNUM, THE GREATEST SHOWMAN

DEBORAH NOYES

CANDLEWICK PRESS

Copyright © 2020 by Deborah Noyes

First edition 2020

Library of Congress Catalog Card Number pending
ISBN 978-0-7636-5981-3

19 20 21 22 23 24 LBM 10 9 8 7 6 5 4 3 2 1

Printed in Melrose Park, IL, U.S.A.

This book was typeset in Golden Cockerell ITC.

Candlewick Press
99 Dover Street
Somerville, Massachusetts 02144

visit us at www.candlewick.com

A JUNIOR LIBRARY GUILD SELECTION

CONTENTS

———◆◆◆———

THE MERMAID (1842)
· 1 ·

THE MYSTERIOUS ARM (1842)
· 21 ·

RETURNING A BLOOM TO ITS BUD (1845)
· 51 ·

BESIDE MYSELF (1851)
· 75 ·

WE WILL ALWAYS BE SISTERS (1852)
· 107 ·

THE FAIRY WEDDING (1863)
· 129 ·

AN EXTRAORDINARY SPECIMEN
OF MAGNIFIED HUMANITY (1865)
· 151 ·

THE BEARDED LADY'S SON (1868)
· 183 ·

IT'S NOT HUMBUG IF YOU BELIEVE IT (1869)
· 205 ·

ALL ELEPHANTS ARE TRAGIC (1889)
· 221 ·

WHAT MAKES YOU THINK
WE WANT YOU HERE? (1891)
· 245 ·

A NOTE ABOUT THE STORIES
· 269 ·

IMAGE CREDITS
· 273 ·

THE MERMAID

The animal was an ugly, dried-up, black-looking, and diminutive specimen, about three feet long. Its mouth was open, its tail turned over, and its arms thrown up, giving it the appearance of having died in great agony.

—P. T. Barnum

Mother snored on the daybed. There was a mermaid swimming just upstairs somewhere, in the museum, and Mother snored.

Caroline lifted her mother's heavy arm to tug out the news sheet, letting it drop again. The mermaid was in the paper today. Daddy's museum was often in the news, but more so since the ladyfish arrived.

Her father had read the article aloud over breakfast. An engraving showed the creature at rest on a rock beside two elegant sister mermaids. She stared into a hand mirror, and her breasts were bare. Caroline knew Mother was scandalized by the set of her mouth and the way she blew on her tea to avoid their eyes. "Questions?" she chirped, in a tone that warned, *don't ask*.

Caroline shrugged. Though she was nine and Helen two, they saw breasts all the time—Mother's, while baby Frances sucked.

When their mother fed Frances right at the breakfast table that morning, Daddy had called her a "fishwife." At first, this confused Caroline. Did he mean Charity Barnum was the ladyfish, the same mermaid on display upstairs? But how? Mother mostly stood by the window or dozed on the daybed, as now, but she never left their sight. And when she unfastened her dressing gown to feed Frances, her bosom did not in any way resemble the graceful mermaids'.

Caroline knew to guard her questions. She would rather solve them herself when she could, and Madge had used the same word last week, only differently. *Fishwife* meant "common," Caroline deduced with pride.

But this morning she had another question, one she couldn't answer herself.

Daddy replied with his back to her, riffling through a pile of contracts. "It's the medicine."

Answers made more questions sometimes, especially Daddy's answers, but with his back to her, he couldn't see her furrowed brow. He had found the page he was looking for and scanned it triumphantly, crushing the paper in his hands. "That's what makes her sleep so much." He looked up sympathetically. "The medicine."

Whatever was on the paper had brightened his mood. Daddy felt sorry for his "wild three," he confided, kneeling by them, but "for the old girl's sake"—he pointed his dimpled chin at Mother on the lounge—"you'll have to keep your voices down today."

He paused over the cradle to fuss with Frances's blanket. Daddy hated baby talk (there was altogether too much "pootsy-wootsy mamby-pamby" spoken to children, he maintained) but resorted to it now to make his point. "Let my girls be doves"—he looked back at them—"and coo like this—*coo, coo, coo*—until she wakes."

Two of three Barnum daughters cooed on

command until Helen broke off, boldly asking the real question: "But *when* will Mother get up?"

A Helen question was a thorn lodged in your thumb. You carried it around until someone saw your discomfort and removed it. Daddy admired her candor—yet another reason Caroline often itched to slap Helen or shake her; however clever she might be, Helen was young enough to fall for the same games over and over. *Look into my hand,* Caroline would coax, opening a fist. *Closer . . . see? You trust me, right?*

Slap, slap.

Daddy tied a silk cravat at his throat. The hired girl would be here soon, he said. Madge came mornings to tidy and heat broth for their lunch. Sometimes, when Frances wailed for no reason and Mother shut herself in her room after Daddy left for the day, Madge bounced the furious infant round the house on her hip. "Colic," she'd say, scowling at Mother's door.

"You said after this week we would never drink broth again," Helen observed with her air of being disappointed in advance. Daddy said it made her sound more like the old men who played chess outside Philosophers' Hall, his favorite barbershop, than a child. "You said we'd dine with the Astors."

"And I am a man of my word."

He chucked Helen's chin—dimpled, like his. Everyone said they looked alike, while Caroline had Mother's sleepy eyes if not her underwater slowness — no mermaid moved like Mother. Mermaids were bullet swift.

Unless you had Daddy's promises in writing, Mother said, he rarely kept them, and anyway he made everything up. Unlike those of the boys in school stories — who tied your braid to the back of your chair — his jokes were on whole cities. All of New York suffered Daddy's whims and hoaxes, and he had crowned himself the Prince of Humbug.

"Receipts tripled this week, my girls." With his document tucked under an arm, he bent to kiss their foreheads. Caroline winced when he gave the cradle a shove so sleeping Frances tipped on roily seas. "Our ladyfish will extend her stay."

Caroline sat on her hands. It did not do to betray enthusiasm. "Please let me see the mermaid?" she blurted. "Is she beautiful like the picture?" She had other questions, too. Were the mermaid's scales as sharp as steel blades? Did you have to cover your ears when she sang or be deafened?

But Mr. Barnum was needed at the office. "Proceeds will not count themselves." He tipped his hat.

"I would like to see the mermaid also," Helen added, almost too quietly to be heard.

Caroline gasped. The audacity. Daddy despised repetition.

But he turned his wrath on *her*, not Helen. He leaned on Caroline's chair arms and nearly knocked his forehead against hers while she held admirably still. "Nownownow," he teased with a mean twinkle in his eye — in the same *tsk* voice he sometimes used on Mother, who withdrew into herself like a duck into its feathers — and out he went, the hall door clicking shut behind him.

Patience is a virtue.

The first-floor apartment, which had once been a billiard hall, felt profoundly hot and stuffy. Caroline scowled at Helen.

In the sitting room, where they waited for Madge while Mother snored, it might have been day or it might have been night.

Caroline put a hand to her heart, as Mother often did, concentrating.

It would be a long morning.

Patience is a virtue.

When the lump in the cradle began to stir, the girls exchanged looks, united in dread.

Caroline rocked Frances with her right hand and lifted the newspaper with her left. The engraved advertisement said the city had "mermaid fever."

Closing her eyes, she imagined the world past the long hallway with its hollow ticking grandfather clock, past the filmy glass of the entryway window.

The street would be full of steaming manure and spit, and a snuffling pig or two. Pretty ladies in bustles and tall bonnets were stepping from carriages, too many to count, with their escorts—one after another, like paper dolls tipping forth from a fathomless black. The museum lived between two worlds, Daddy liked to say. It lured fashionable customers from uptown right alongside people from the Bowery tenements and Five Points.

She could hear his brass band making a clamor on the balcony. Above that, on the roof of the museum, people would be lining up for ice cream. But inside—oh, inside!—there were serpent charmers, ropedancers, glassblowers, and industrious fleas. There was a Gypsy fortune-teller and a professor of phrenology who read your skull by feeling the bumps on your head. This and a ladyfish . . . right upstairs. Yet Caroline Cordelia Barnum (and Helen), the proprietor's own flesh and blood, had never even been inside.

Daddy had no trouble boasting about everything they were missing, especially at bedtime, though the evening ritual of parting was more satisfying than the morning's.

Daddy always tucked them in at night, and his excuses were better than a storybook. "You will kindly forgive Mr. Barnum," he would say, "proprietor of the American Museum, who must now slip away to see to the important work of lighting up the night sky."

While she and Helen waited to fall asleep each night, they watched the beam of his Drummond light circle Broadway, sweeping the street below and the front and sides of the museum. It crept in their window, slashed the ceiling, and turned dizzy circles before retreating again.

Mr. Barnum's other important work, he reminded them — covering first Helen and then Caroline to the chin with their blankets — was to tuck in the animals.

There were huge placards all around the outside of the museum, and it was Helen's job, at this point in the ritual, to make Daddy list the animals they advertised: orangutan and polar bear, elephant and ostrich, camel leopard, tapir, pelican, eagle, gnu, lion, kangaroo, peacock, elk, rattlesnake, tiger, fur seal, and cormorant.

She had memorized the menagerie in a particular order, every animal, and made him start over if he omitted anyone.

When Daddy didn't have time for a proper goodnight, he would tuck them in with the museum catalog for their bedtime book, inviting them to imagine, in their dreams, the midnight snuffling and turning of creatures and the soft bickering of giants and dwarfs playing cards. "And when you wake up," he would say with his big laugh, "I'll be at the table waiting."

He was.

And he promised that on the day they finally got upstairs to visit his "wilderness of realities," they would have the whole of five floors to themselves, and the mermaid, too.

They would watch the sun go down from the roof deck.

They would be served cake with buttercream icing and dishes of cherry ice cream.

They would cheer the fireworks.

But not today.

Today they were stuck at home again, with baby Frances fixing to wake up and wail.

Caroline set down the newspaper and rocked the cradle even harder, with all her might, but the bundle now thrashing in slow motion began to whimper.

That's how it started, as if someone were plucking its lip (Caroline still thought of Frances as an "it") like a string on a guitar. Then came a soft sputter that escalated into an alarming, mind-numbing yowl from which there was no escape until Mother stuffed a nipple in its mouth.

It couldn't hold up the head lolling on the pile of rolled fat that was its neck. It had a red face and, under downy hair, a scabby scalp. Frances wasn't an *entirely* ugly baby, not anymore. She had grown into herself and had an elfin, pretty form. Mother called her a sprite. But she — it — was shiftless and greedy like all babies, and there was something growing up in her eyes that Caroline didn't like.

As little sisters went, Helen was a nuisance, but she could keep still and occupy herself. Frances always seemed hungry — all sucking mouth and beady eyes — and unsatisfied, no matter how often she was fed or changed. Her infant hunger was in her whole being, not just her belly, and now the sputtering became gasps, the urgent little lungs sucking in air. Any moment, that air would exit as a wail.

"Your turn, Helen," Caroline snapped, and let the cradle fall still as the wailing began. They both stared down helplessly.

Helen lifted the tin of matches from the mantel and dropped it in the cradle. Two red fists caught the make-shift rattle and shook, spilling wooden matches all over the crocheted blanket. The sputtering escalated.

"Don't!" Caroline seized the tin. "She'll burn the museum down!"

The little fists flailed, knocking Caroline's wrists and knuckles. She sighed, pinching matches from the fabric. "Mother," she said coolly, "Frances is awake."

Caroline returned the matchbox to the mantel, crossed her arms, and waited for their mother to stir from her stupor. "I know you hear me," she added under her breath.

Helen's eyes widened.

Mother rolled toward them, her banana curls shamelessly flattened on one side. Her face looked old, and there was a painful crease from the upholstery on her cheek. "Hand her," she murmured.

Loosening her gown, Mother took Frances and rolled over with her.

There was a mermaid upstairs.

Caroline (and Helen) wanted to see it.

Caroline wanted to see all that the catalog called "monstrous, scaly, and strange," from the trained chickens and the dog that operated a knitting machine to the puppets and the python.

It was their own museum, and Daddy had promised, repeatedly, but he was too busy.

Mother must have felt them both at her back, cooing in their thoughts, biding their time until Madge arrived to fix lunch. "Thank you, girls," she murmured to the wall, and Caroline had never heard a voice so hoarse and thick with sorrow.

Frances would suck and sleep.

Mother, who evaded the topic of the museum altogether, would sleep.

The arrows of the hands would move round and round the face of the sun on the grandfather clock.

On the hour, the clock's bell would chime and fall silent.

Caroline walked back to Helen and took her by the hand. She tugged her out to the kitchen. "I have a plan." She knelt to whisper.

*   *   *

She had to give Helen credit for stealth and daring. They were as quiet as pantry mice. Helen did as she was told and took the coins from the milkman's can, then tucked them into her slipper. It was hot and bright and loud out on the street. Once they were through the door, Helen gripped Caroline's hand so hard her bones creaked, but her big, bright eyes darted everywhere, looking for the animals. Caroline felt her sister's leaping pulse in the hollow between her thumb and pointer finger.

It was a Saturday, and the entrance line wound around the block.

Hot sun beat down on them — she had rushed them out without even their bonnets — as they huddled together listening to the murmur of conversations all around, families, mainly, with rough Bowery boys hanging on the rail and a few lone men, one of whom — a fellow with a meaty nose and a stain on his lapel — eyed them grimly.

A sheen of sweat shone over Helen's freckles, and Caroline itched in her indoor gown, too warm for open sunlight. They had no parasol, but at least she had thought to bring the exhibition catalog. She kept it tucked under an arm until she could no longer ignore the feeling that everyone, not just Mr. Meaty Nose, was staring at them, at which point she opened the program and flipped through, pointing things out to Helen, the secret things they would see and hear and touch and smell.

They were collared just inside the door. *Collared* was a word Caroline especially liked and had always wanted to use in a sentence. But she was too nervous, just now, to enjoy it.

"I know you." The man laughed and waved them over to his seat on a tall stool by the ticket counter, where he waited for the early-morning receipts to be bagged. It was Daddy's partner-in-crime, as Mother called him, Mr. Lyman.

Stepping closer to the counter, Caroline held out their coins in a trembling hand.

"I don't want your money." Mr. Lyman leaned forward and hooked a thumb toward the mysterious expanse behind them. "*He* might. But I don't."

Caroline laughed because he seemed to require it of her. Helen laughed because Caroline did.

"No chaperone today?" Mr. Lyman asked, eyeing Mr. Meaty Nose in line behind them.

"Mother was . . . sleeping," Caroline explained in a small voice.

A woman behind them began to complain that they were taking too long. They were holding up the line, and what were two little girls doing out alone like that, anyway? The two rough boys who had been hanging on the rail whistled through their fingers. Mr. Lyman was forced to walk round and take both girls by the hand. He excused himself to the man in the ticket booth, then led them upstairs to Daddy's office.

As Mr. Lyman pulled them through the crowds, Caroline's heart beat so hard she thought it would deafen her. Her limbs felt quavery, and she couldn't see Helen on the other side. Seeing Helen, meeting her steady gaze, always gave Caroline nerve, but her nerves were failing now. She was done for.

Daddy glanced up from his ledger.

"Mother was asleep." It was all Caroline could think to say. She stared at her shoes, pigeon-toed.

Helen did likewise, in house slippers.

"I'm sorry," Caroline offered. They had never in their lives gone out unattended or stolen milk money or any money, much less employed deceit.

She knew he was cross, because he said nothing. Not one word. He kept scribbling in his ledger.

They were wasting his valuable time.

He should be counting receipts.

She felt a moment's terror and trembling, but he didn't shout or scold or cuff them. He stood up slowly, walked round the desk, and knelt—Daddy was very tall—to lift her chin. He asked, "What took you so long?"

"Levi!" he called, and Mr. Lyman, who had been hovering outside the office door, returned with peaked eyebrows. Daddy nudged them forward, a hand on the back of each girl's neck. "As you know, these are chips off the old block. I'll take them up to see the mermaid after I'm through here. Please escort them to the sitting room to wait."

Even Helen knew not to speak at so sacred a time. Caroline felt wise and very old, though Mr. Lyman again took her hand like a baby's — and Helen's in the other. "Brace yourselves, girls," he said, laughing over a shoulder.

Daddy winked before they walked away, brushing at a splatter of ink from his pen. "We reward initiative here."

The sofa they waited on had supported numberless backsides. The quiet room had high ceilings and exotic landscapes, fruits, and birds painted on the walls. They could see the main entrance hall through a wide threshold, and the lumbering flow of visitors bumping and jostling. Caroline thought she saw one of the rough boys go by, but in that crush of humanity there were no faces, only hats and bonnets, sharp elbows and shoulders.

At first, the girls observed propriety, their backs straight, hands folded (though gloveless and exposed) on their knees, ankles tucked under long skirts. It was hard for Caroline to judge the passing of time with no grandfather clock to help. Moments became hours. She missed Mother. She even missed Frances.

Helen shifted onto her side and pulled her legs up in unladylike fashion. She laid her head in Caroline's lap to nap, forcing Caroline to smooth her sister's dress down and down for modesty's sake. Helen was not heavy, but Caroline's legs grew numb and tingling under her weight. Defiance plagued her again. This was what Mother would do. Sit by and sigh and close her eyes, watching the magic lantern show inside her skull.

Helen whimpered in a dream.

What if they went up on their own?

But the memory of Daddy's face as he knelt to lift her chin, his pride in their adventurousness, gave Caroline pause. His pride would become irritation or anger if they suffered a mishap or disappointed him in one of countless ways. Caroline couldn't let him down after pleasing him so well without quite understanding how.

Just as she, too, was beginning to doze off, Madge appeared above her like a harpy from a nightmare, jostling them awake.

"Your mother is worried sick!"

Both girls sat up and stretched. Everything hurt.

"Your *poor* mother," Madge droned on.

"He forgot us, didn't he?" Caroline asked with as much dignity as she could muster.

"He was detained. He sent for me. Come now; look sharp. I have babies of my own to tend."

Caroline wanted to say *I am not a baby*, but that would be sass. Instead, in a voice even more proud and disinterested than before, she repeated, "We only wanted to see the mermaid."

"Yes, I know. It's on the way out." Madge sniffed and seized and released Helen's wrist. "Let's go."

They hurried through the halls after Madge. In her drab brown coat, she was like a bird in an autumn bush, easy to lose sight of among such color and pattern. Their legs were short, and it took only a few moments to lose sight of Madge altogether. Everything was loud and bright, and Caroline had to stop and let it go by, let everything go by.

Helen stopped short, clasping her leader's hand so hard it hurt. Mirror tears streamed down her round face. Caroline wrested her hand free, and Helen sank to the floor. She seized Caroline's leg as if it were the trunk of a tree. "Stop, Helen! Let me think!"

"Are you lost, young lady?"

Another voice, leaning close with peppermint breath: "What's your name, dear?"

I am Barnum, Caroline Cordelia Barnum! This is my very own museum, all five floors. Every seashell and tiger belongs to me, and so does the one-and-only club that killed Captain Cook....

But her mouth only moved like a fish's.

A small crowd had gathered, as if she and Helen were human oddities in their own right, and the ruckus brought Madge back to them. Huffing, she caught them up by the sleeves and steered them past the gawkers, out of one hall and into the next, and from there it went by in a sickening blur, the Tattooed Man and the Highland Mammoth Boys. A loud voice narrated the manner in which Mr. Nellis, the Armless Wonder, used his feet to load and fire a pistol and shoot with a

bow and arrow (or, "in the season of Cupid," called the
barker, cut paper "valentines") . . .

Madge steered them here and there, not gently,
until they came to a small viewing room with a sign
reading *The Fejee Mermaid*. Caroline wanted to pause
reverently and compose herself, but Madge and Helen
had no such impulse, and no right to see the mermaid
first, so Caroline swiped at a stray tear, and in they went.

The creature was in a tall glass dome on a stand. She
would never again comb her curls or skim the waves or
shoot like a bullet through the depths.

"There is your mermaid," Madge said in her sour,
scolding voice; there was also a hint of satisfaction,
which frightened Caroline — that a grown person in
charge of their well-being should despise them so.
What had they done to deserve it?

The creature looked starved and shrunken, like
blackened earwax, carved into the shape of a fish below
and a monkey, or a tiny old woman with shriveled
breasts, above.

"You may as well know sooner than late." Madge
leveled her gaze on Caroline, *someone else's spoiled child*.
"There are no mermaids."

Helen had stepped very close, her nose almost to
the glass, or what she could reach of it. Caroline kept
her distance, and one eye on the ugly beast, trying to
think what it reminded her of.

Mother. It reminded her of their mother, curled

toward the wall, frozen in her pose like a cursed thing from a fairy story.

Caroline felt no fear, no pity for the ladyfish, only amazement, as her father intended. This was, after all, Daddy's mermaid. A rush of good cheer overcame her. Pugnacious optimism was a trait she and her father shared. Caroline took Helen by the hand before they could be bullied forward again, and cupped her other to her sister's seashell ear. "Let's go home," she said with a disdainful glance at Madge. "There are no *real* mermaids here."

THE MYSTERIOUS ARM

I took great pains to train my diminutive prodigy, devoting many hours to that purpose, by day and by night, and succeeded, because he had native talent and an intense love of the ludicrous. He became very fond of me. I was, and yet am, sincerely attached to him.

—P. T. Barnum

1842, BRIDGEPORT, CONNECTICUT

Once upon a time there was a tiny man who sold kisses.

That tiny man grew rich beyond imagining, but on this day he wasn't special yet. He was an ordinary if very little boy in a saltbox house marching a tin soldier along a windowsill.

Charlie could see over the sill but just. His mouth fogged the glass, but he made out his ma and Mrs. Fairchild, huddled in their cloaks. Father set down his wheelbarrow and joined them. All their lips moved at once, breathing frost.

Ma looked back at Charlie in the window, where he was playing the game of crossing and uncrossing his eyes—focusing first on his own pale reflection and then on his elders—to and fro in a kind of struggle.

It was so cold in Albany that November day that the Hudson River froze. All river transport stopped, and the showman who would change Charlie Stratton's life had to take the rattling Housatonic Railroad instead.

The train stopped in Bridgeport, where Barnum lodged the night with his half brother, Philo, who kept the Franklin House. Over supper, talk turned to an extraordinarily small boy in town. The showman made inquiries and sent Philo to fetch the specimen from his family's little saltbox house at the edge of the village near the Pequannock River.

When Charlie entered the smoky tavern with his parents, Mr. Barnum stood to greet them. Charlie didn't reach the man's knees.

With the showman regarding them intensely and all eyes staring, Ma began to stammer and wring her hands. Their son had stopped growing when he was seven months old, she told the tavern, though all the locals knew already. The doctor didn't know why.

The tiny boy with bright eyes hid behind his mother's skirts as they followed Philo Barnum to a table.

"Say hello to Mr. Barnum, Charlie," Sherwood Stratton urged his son.

The rascal emerged by degrees and shook hands all around.

It fast became apparent that while the parents were dullards, young Stratton was both clever and charming. The showman couldn't believe his luck.

Food arrived, and the party ate quietly. After smacking his lips and folding his napkin, the weary youngster climbed into his ma's lap. There he sat for the rest of the interview, enjoying the clack of his heels against her chair leg.

Cynthia Stratton tried to muffle the noise in her palms, even tried trapping her son's tiny knees between her own, bunching her plaid skirts, but Charlie kicked all the harder until the showman leaned close. Would Charlie like to go for a walk? Just the two of them?

Happily bewildered, the boy let himself be led to the door without a coat. He hopped down the tavern steps at the big man's side, admiring a snow squall and tipping his head back to catch feathery flakes on his tongue.

"Would you like to be large one day, young man? Far and away larger than life? With your name shouted on posters around the world?"

"Charlie?"

The showman stopped in his snow tracks. "Why, no," he admitted. "That won't do. But a rose by any other name ..."

Charlie pinched his nose, enjoying how it changed his voice. "I don't want to be a rose."

"Fussy things," the big man agreed. "But a general? You'd like to be a general?"

Charlie shook the outstretched thumb while snow tumbled around the mismatched pair, and the deal was struck.

Charles Stratton was no more.

"We'll count the venture an experiment for now," Mr. Barnum told Pa, who saw his only son as an embarrassment.

With Mrs. Stratton's blessing, Sherwood Stratton agreed to lease the fruit of his loins for three dollars a week plus room, board, and traveling expenses, to give the youngster the life and "stature" (Mr. Barnum winked down at Charlie, as if the word marked a secret between them) he wouldn't otherwise enjoy.

In early December, the showman and his discovery, parents in tow, boarded the steamship *Nimrod* and chugged through Long Island Sound. With no pillow to sit on, the tiny man could only look up at clouds hurtling past. His size often made his surroundings a mystery. Sometimes he tugged Ma's sleeve, and she lifted him into her lap. But when distracted, as now, she set her jaw against him, and the world above remained a puzzle.

At New York Harbor, in a swirl of rigging, shouts, and burly longshoremen heaving sacks and trunks, they hailed a hackney cab.

After the dirt and drab of provincial Bridgeport, New York—or what Charlie could see of it—was a teeming carnival. It shocked him that such a place existed, making his mind turn and turn. What else lay hidden?

The family's new home, the American Museum, sat on wide, bustling Broadway. Damp paving stone polished by the tread of feet shone in the gaslight. Brick made a velvet curtain behind all the movement: omnibuses, hackney cabs, coaches, carriages, and people—far too many to count, in all sizes, shapes, and colors.

But none his size.

Charlie and his parents would lodge on the fifth floor of the museum with the other performers. The

rooms were well equipped and comfortable, Ma pronounced, inspecting each fork and teacup twice.

Pa sat on gnarled carpenter's hands on the bed while
their neighbors squabbled behind thin walls. They were
giants (or more-than-usually giant)—one French and
one Arabian—who lived on either side of the hall and,
the family had been warned, liked a boisterous game of
cards. Reportedly there were "little people," too, folks
closer to Charlie's size.

Their sponsor and his "esteemed brood" lived in a
converted billiard hall below the museum, where the
tiny man's education would commence the following
morning.

While Pa contemplated his worn boots, Ma
watched the night-lit city and the slashing beam of Mr.
Barnum's Drummond light through the window.

The Strattons were a long way from home, and the
tiny man was not sorry.

They were, as Mr. Barnum had predicted in his
sidelong whisper in the Bridgeport tavern, on the brink
of a great adventure.

"We'll get to the point, you and I," the showman said in
the morning. He laid a mirror on the floor beside the
roaring hearth. "That's for you. To observe your progress," he said. "Call me Mr. B., and I'll call you Tom."

That day, Tom learned that his new name came
from a story. Tom Thumb was a knight of King Arthur's

Round Table, one so tiny he rode a mouse and battled spiders. There were other performers in New York and vaudeville who went by the name, Mr. B. explained, some nearly as tiny as he was, but none were generals.

General Tom Thumb liked to be read to, and it became the custom for Mr. B. to share tales and verse and bits of whimsy before rehearsals. He studied Tom's face while he absorbed it all, the rhythm and the color; soon Tom would feel the words changing him as hot air changes the shape and prospects of a balloon.

But that first morning, Tom accepted a plum and a biscuit on a saucer and took his seat by the fire, kicking the chair legs nervously. He had what Ma called "the butterflies" until a glimpse of his reflection in the mirror on the floor calmed him. He stuck out his tongue at the other Tom and bit into his plum, slurping sweet juice.

After breakfast, Mr. B. taught him to strut and salute. Tom filled himself with wind and marched so stoutly that his knees brushed his chin. He jutted chest and elbows and sang a sea shanty while Mr. B. smiled. The teacher's bright eyes tracked him, distant as stars but comforting, too, as only stars can be.

"Try this." Mr. B. lifted Tom onto a table and fetched an ivory-tipped walking cane. "Grab hold."

Tom seized the cane below the hook and felt a dizzy rapture as Mr. B. lifted him off the table into the air. The showman marched a dangling Tom round the room, and the big man and the tiny one cackled in unison.

"You raised the roof," Mrs. B. complained during a lunch of cold beef sandwiches that day. It was just the three of them, and Mr. B. couldn't stop smiling.

In weeks to come, Tom would learn to play dress-up and dance, dash off quips and comebacks, and sing "Yankee Doodle" in his piping treble. Mr. B. coached him hour after hour, day after day, sometimes long into the night. "Say when you tire," he offered, but he didn't mean it, and Tom had plenty of practice appearing brighter and bigger and faster than he was. You had no choice, at his size, but to look sharp and keep pace.

Tom trailed the merry showman like a puppy, imitating his swagger. He could copy Mr. B.'s voice exactly (or even, he learned, mock the sorrowful harping of Mrs. B. and not earn a scolding for it). The mischief he liked best brought him only applause, and soon, Mr. B. said, they would all profit from it.

On the best days — before Mr. B. noticed and dispatched them — the Barnum daughters crowded behind the door and peeked through the crack. Tom didn't know their names, only that there were three.

When their father left the room to accept a caller or a letter, the girls sometimes spilled in. The oldest was given to fits of giggling at the slightest provocation and easily spooked by footfalls. ("If I ran a smithy shop," her father had barked at her the first day, "would you lurk by the forge? You would not. Nor will you disrupt my business now.")

The *"enfant terrible,"* as Mr. B. called his youngest, was only slightly larger than Tom and reminded him of the hummingbird that used to come suck the red flowers in his ma's garden. She was small and impish, like him, with a pert nose and mischievous eyes, and seemed to vibrate in a way you couldn't see but only feel.

The middle sister, still and watchful, was the puzzle Tom liked best. He couldn't help stealing glances at her — her name was Helen, he would learn — and her cool, unflinching eyes stared back. She always looked alert but with a queenly dignity, even in a dress much plainer than her older sister's. Because Tom couldn't guess how to make her laugh, Mr. B.'s middle daughter was a mystery.

One day, as Tom was being fitted for costumes in the sitting room, he looked up at just the right moment. The door to the hall was open a crack, and through it he glimpsed an arm, a stealthy blue arm, and the blue let in a flash of pink that streaked to the far wall and wriggled behind a tapestry.

While the tailor circled, taking Tom's measurements, Frances stayed hidden, but with the man's back to her, she peeped out and thumbed her nose at Tom, glancing toward the hall for approval.

Standing tall on the tabletop, Tom tried to maintain the manly pose Mr. B. favored for the French general

Napoleon. It would become Tom's most famous role. (For Romulus, Tom would have a helmet and spear, for Cupid a bow and arrow, and for Cain a club to slay Abel with, but it was the general's wide hat Tom fancied most.)

He was disappointed to learn that his opening-day schedule excluded singing and jesting. Mr. B. approved just one routine. Tom could dance a Highland fling as a Scottish chieftain (dirk and claymore with powder horn and deer knife). That was all.

Tom wouldn't be playing a hero, Mr. B. explained, but the *statue* of a hero. His goal, for now, was to stand perfectly still on a stone pillar. If he showed discipline, active roles would follow.

Frances bobbed out from behind the tapestry, and Tom's mouth twitched. This was his chance to prove his discipline, but the *enfant terrible* began a clumsy dance, lifting her skirts and kicking her little feet high, only to get a boot tangled in the drapery. The heavy curtain and rod crashed down, burying Frances in a heap. At the same moment, Tom moved, and the tailor stuck him with a pin.

Mr. B. left his writing desk in the alcove to pull the squirming intruder out from the velvet. He set her in the now empty hall, clapped the door closed, and turned the lock.

Frances was known for her tempers, and something out there, a vase or planter, crashed to the parquet.

"The inmates are running the asylum," Mr. B. complained to the tailor, who asked through the line of thread between his lips, "How ever did she reach the doorknob?"

It was a tall door, Tom conceded, with an ornate brass knob. He had been let through it like a lapdog.

"Frances has her ways."

There was a hint of pride in the father's voice, but Tom had seen the blue arm. He knew better.

Tom should have been relieved. He could practice being a block of stone in peace. But Frances and the mysterious arm had left a hollow in the room. Tom had never had friends his own age. Other children didn't trust him, but the Misses B. were not ordinary children.

That night Tom was invited with his parents and some of Mr. B.'s associates to dine with the Barnums in their apartment.

At the other end of the table, over custard and shortbread, Mr. B. caught Tom's parents up on their progress. "I've taken the boy under my wing," he boasted, "but the credit is Tom's." That a young child should learn so much so quickly, the showman admitted — with lightning wit, comic timing, and muscle control to boot — was astonishing even to him.

Pa coughed into his fist. He was happy to celebrate Tom's "deformity" now that it turned a profit, but in

Bridgeport he'd been indifferent at best . . . mortified at worst.

Mr. B. reached back for a pile of broadsheets, advertisements for Tom's exhibition. They were "rolling off the presses," he said, circulating the pages though none had asked him to. "'ONLY FIFTEEN POUNDS!'" he recited. "'Perfectly symmetrical in all his proportions! Intelligent and graceful beyond belief, and SMALLER THAN ANY INFANT that ever walked alone!'"

He spoke the exclamation points, and his associates murmured agreement. Caroline, at her father's left elbow, glared down at her plate while Frances (who usually took her meals in the kitchen with Cook) clapped wildly in her high chair, delighted by her father's manic energy. The excitement was wearing on her and her oldest sister equally, though at opposite extremes.

Over the past week, with Tom's debut drawing near, Caroline had grown hostile. This evening alone, she had gone out of her way to criticize his table manners. Tom had worked hard to hold his fork just so — such a large fork! — and winced at her words, but Helen leaned in beside him, and her blue sleeve brushed his. "Caro's just jealous of all the attention you get," she soothed. "Pay no mind."

Helen's sleeve was powder blue with a royal sheen.

Tom turned his face to smile at no one, a ridiculous toothy grin. He was glad there was no mirror here, as there was on the floor in the sitting room when they rehearsed.

Farther down the table, Mrs. B. fanned herself with her napkin. Helen cupped her hand to his ear again. "Caro sounds more like Mother every day," she said, "and I'll say so at bedtime. Don't worry. I tell her every chance I get."

After that, as usual, she remained queenly and aloof, but her hazel eyes brimmed with pleasure.

The Strattons gaped at the type on the advertisements bearing their son's likeness:

P. T. BARNUM OF THE AMERICAN MUSEUM, BROADWAY AT ANN STREET, IS PROUD TO ANNOUNCE THAT HE HAS IMPORTED FROM LONDON TO ADD TO HIS COLLECTION OF EXTRAORDINARY CURIOSITIES FROM ALL OVER THE WORLD, THE RAREST, TINIEST, THE MOST DIMINUTIVE DWARF IMAGINABLE, ENGAGED AT EXTRAORDINARY EXPENSE — TOM THUMB, ELEVEN YEARS OLD AND ONLY TWENTY-FIVE INCHES HIGH!

"E-le-ven?" stammered Tom's ma. "*London?* Why on *earth?*"

Mr. B. explained that all four-year-olds are small, things being relative. Without a bit of "puff," the true wonder of Tom's person would escape the public. "Not to mention," he said, "we'll profit from the American fancy for all things exotic."

Egged on by the Strattons, who took it all in

hungrily, Mr. B. read aloud from the pamphlet that would accompany their son's exhibition: "'When General Tom Thumb was just a babe,'" he read, "'Nature put a veto on his further upward progress.'"

It was his favorite line, Tom knew, and Mr. B. laughed out loud, bushy eyebrows peaking. "Most people can't fathom he's just e-le-ven"—he glanced wryly at Ma—"much less younger. Here's to our general." He raised his glass, and a hearty clinking began.

Tom would remember the toasts and salutations around the table that night (even Caroline clapped, once and grudgingly) for years—long after the applause of the masses grew faint and mundane.

When General Tom Thumb took the stage in the museum's Hall of Living Curiosities over the winter holidays, New York went wild.

Reviewers fueled Mr. B.'s publicity machine: with hands the size of half-dollars, they wrote, and feet just three inches long, Tom was "the greatest little mortal alive," a "perfect little gentleman."

Their star was on the rise, and the museum hummed with excitement. As business boomed, Mr. B. and his cronies, the other performers, Tom's parents, and even Caroline began to treat him differently, though Tom couldn't have explained how. He knew only that he felt more at ease in the little sitting room in the apartment than anywhere else.

Helpless to squelch the enthusiasm of Frances (and Helen — Caroline no longer graced them with her presence), Mr. B. now let the girls visit before and after rehearsal blocks.

Tom and Frances liked to stretch on the hearth rug, propped on their elbows, and kick their legs. Frances's pink face held a sheen of exertion no matter what she was doing, bangs mashed to her damp forehead, and this morning she was making little half-audible sounds in her throat, perhaps humming.

Stationed by the window as always, Helen remained quiet and self-possessed, radiating approval she wouldn't voice. Frances was Helen's particular pet, and Frances loved Tom, so they seemed to rhyme, the three of them, to ring in tune.

Frances had the limited vocabulary of any toddler but blurted out "Cat!" pointing into the flames. She glanced back, and Helen nodded sagely from her window station, but Frances wanted more. One hand became a grasping claw, signaling mutely for her sister. *Come down at once*, it commanded. Helen only lifted the curtain, but Frances began to whimper, opening and closing the hand furiously. Helen hushed her and knelt, stretching alongside them with a resigned air.

It was such a pleasure to see Helen at eye level that Tom had to look away. He squinted into the fire. "Cat," he said, making bug eyes to indicate surprise. Frances squirmed with joy. (He saw it, too!) She kicked her legs harder.

For most of Tom's life, his tininess had amused others, but it had little to do with him. Tom had not earned their mirth. His littleness had. Frances (and Helen) may have been the first to enjoy Tom for his own sake.

Making the two Misses B. laugh felt like his true work, the role he was made for.

"Fish," he challenged, his finger tracing the shape from the leaping flames.

"Fish!" Frances clapped. She cheered for the fish and found a bird.

Tom offered a bear, and so it went.

"She knows the names of all the animals," Helen whispered proudly.

"You taught her?"

"I did. When she's older, we'll study their Latin names. I'm making a survey."

"You can read?"

"Of course," Helen said breezily. "Can't you?"

"I'm learning," Tom admitted, "but I like to be read to."

"I'll read to you."

"You will?"

"Of course, Charlie."

"Bear! Bear! Bear!" screamed Frances.

Nobody said *of course* like Helen. Nobody called him Charlie, either, not anymore. Not for a long time.

* * *

"You're doing well, my boy," Mr. B. announced later that morning—to cheer him, Tom supposed, after turning the others out so they could work. "I have good news."

Tom looked up, hopeful.

"I'm going to try you out in the lecture hall tonight."

The lecture hall was actually a large theater. Tom would take the stage at last.

But somehow it didn't make him as happy as he'd imagined it would.

During performances sweet with the smells of peppermint, orange peel, and sugar doughnuts from the concession stand, Tom let his mind drift while Mr. B. enacted the ritual of selecting a little boy from the crowd ("Scale is everything," he liked to say, "all things being relative") and walking him up onstage to compare his size with Tom's.

"I'd rather have a little miss," Tom squeaked on cue with an exaggerated wink, when they arrived, and the audience—every audience—howled with laughter while the child from the crowd, a giant by Tom's standards, slumped onstage and blushed.

Sending the biggest draw at the museum away on tour was a risk, but Mr. B. often did—in the company of Sherwood Stratton or the museum's business manager. Tom went willingly, though travel made him melancholy. It confirmed the strangeness that he had always felt at the heart of the world but that the world reflected back as his own.

Trained to speak and act like a man, Tom took wine with his meals. He puffed on the cigars grown men offered him with a smile. He spent six weeks on the road that spring, doing his "statues" and the occasional song-and-dance routine. He swaggered, staggered, and marched around stage at Moses Kimball's museum in Boston and other places, and rarely tired despite long hours and almost ceaseless labor.

"You're doing well, my boy," Mr. B. assured him, as ever, when he returned, but Tom felt too tired to smile.

"Would you like a present?"

Tom thought hard, but all he could see in his mind's eye was Frances (and Helen), and he was afraid to ask because perhaps, this time, the showman would say no. Mr. B. would fold his arms and that would be the end of it.

Frances (and Helen), who had grown very large in Tom's thoughts while he was on tour — much larger than life — could never be restored to him in their former glory. Tom might be a teeny-tiny child, but he was also what Mr. B. called "an old soul." He already knew he would miss the way Frances hung on his neck like a monkey while he dragged her, with difficulty, along the carpet. He would miss playing knight to her horse. More than anything, he would miss the look on Helen's face while she watched their antics from afar.

But his education was complete now, and their time together in the apartment in the old billiard hall below the museum would fade like a dream. Life was just too busy.

Tom was rarely invited downstairs anymore but took meals upstairs in the suite with his parents or with patrons determined to "wine and dine" him. He would not be allowed to idle all morning by the fire, even as the star and savior — according to Mr. B., in private — of P. T. Barnum's American Museum. Tom had yet to grow into the savvy businessman he would become, and it was not his way to bully or complain, though he steeled himself to say, "I would like a ball of twine. Please."

"A ball of twine?"

"Yes. *Please.*" Tom sat with crossed arms, resolute, adding in a near whisper, "And a visit with Frances (and Helen)."

Mr. B. summoned Caroline and sent her in search of twine. While they waited, he filled Tom in on plans for their European tour. The contracts had been reviewed by his parents and signed, and they would depart at the new year.

Caroline delivered the twine and skulked out again — such errands were beneath her — as her father shouted for the others.

Frances scrambled in like a wild animal through a grate, while Helen entered with proud determination, as if ready to be turned out again.

Mr. B. excused himself to see to the day's accounts. "Play with your ball of twine," he instructed Tom over his shoulder. It was one of many moments of perfect understanding between them.

Tom and Frances set to work with one mind, winding the twine around chair and table legs low to the ground until the room was a web of peril, a trap for those too tall to know better. Helen smiled her lofty smile by the window, regarding their work out of the corner of her eye.

Mr. B. made a show of tripping over their handiwork repeatedly when he returned, sending the room into paroxysms of delight. Tom and Frances howled and rolled on the carpet. Helen kept her composure but had to cover her mouth to do so.

Hot and exhausted from the work, Tom and Frances sat face-to-face on their knees. Mr. B. blew on the ink of the document he had been writing. Tom searched for Helen over her sister's shoulder. Their eyes locked as Frances bobbed up and began to wind Tom in twine, circling him while he played the straight man for once.

"Frances . . ." Mr. B. folded his letter into an envelope, sealed it with wax, and nodded to Helen. "It's time for Tom to work now."

The imp puffed out her cheeks, but Helen reached for her. Taking the hand, Frances let herself be led through the door without protest as Helen backed out slowly. Tom would remember that ghosting smile of Helen's always.

When the day came for the ocean crossing, a cold day in January of 1844, there was a parade to the port. Mr. B. was so animated, so busy, that Tom didn't dare ask where Frances (and Helen) were and why they had not been allowed to see him off. He felt tragic and abandoned, though every bit of the fanfare was for him.

As the procession passed down Fulton Street, led by the City Brass Band, thousands of women and girls in pretty dresses waved handkerchiefs from their windows and doors. To Tom's bleary eyes, the hankies flapped like white doves with lassoed legs. He bowed gracefully from the open barouche.

"Good-bye to small thinking," Mr. B. shouted into Tom's ear (a perfect small seashell, he had been told at dinner last night by an heiress whose breath smelled of wine) as their party pushed through the throngs at the pier.

Masts and rigging swayed and flapped overhead. Mr. B. grasped the hands of friends and well-wishers as they boarded the ship, and he seemed to swell with emotion when the band struck up "Home, Sweet Home." He was uncharacteristically sentimental on deck, too, as the *Yorkshire* chugged away amid the shrieks of wheeling seagulls. He tousled Tom's hair with one hand. "I'll miss the museum," he said with icy breath.

Tom nodded up at him without speaking (perplexed that it was a building he would miss, not a face, not their faces) as the city grew small and the waves far below pitched against the side of the ship.

Besides the sky, there was nothing — nothing in the world — bigger than the sea.

The tiny man and the showman — together with Tom's parents and tutor, the museum's French naturalist, and a great many trunks — arrived in Liverpool eighteen days later.

Mr. B. would not let the public glimpse his sensation before their opening. Huffing and puffing and flanked by the others, Ma smuggled Tom into the Waterloo Hotel bundled as a baby, a theme they would replay many times during the tour.

Mr. B. had engaged the Egyptian Hall in London's Piccadilly, where the act's popularity built slowly; British "midgets" had played London fairs and sideshows for ages and weren't news, but night after night, "Yankee" General Tom Thumb (in a brown-velvet jacket with brass buttons) worked his magic, and Mr. B. put the spin on it.

Lines of people snaked around the block for tickets. Ladies mobbed the souvenir booth after shows. The receipts rolled in, and Mr. B. maintained that it would change their lives — change them — forever.

One night, ticket holders arrived to find a sign nailed to the door of Egyptian Hall:

CLOSED THIS EVENING,
GENERAL TOM THUMB BEING AT BUCKINGHAM PALACE
BY COMMAND OF HER MAJESTY

Tom had been coached, but he forgot how to address the great lady. He called her "ma'am" rather than "Your Majesty." He licked his butter knife at table. Queen Vic — as Mr. B. called her in private — took no offense and found Tom so delightful she invited him back.

"I have done as no American before me," Mr. B. boasted. "Visited the queen at her palace twice within eight days."

Her Royal Highness received the General with great pleasure, and since everyone wanted to do as Her Majesty did, have what Her Majesty had, love what Her Majesty loved, everyone loved Tom. It became unfashionable, unpatriotic even, not to seek him out and heap gifts and homage upon him. Carriages of the nobility, sixty at a time, crowded the door of their lodgings in Piccadilly. Egyptian Hall was packed for every show. Tom's portraits appeared everywhere.

"You're doing well, my boy."

Mr. B. was so pleased with Tom that he blocked out a day for a shopping spree. "You deserve a reward," he said, but the spree was to reward them both, Tom understood. Mr. B. was forever searching for wonders to populate the museum, but Tom was in a position to insist they devote at least part of the day to finding the perfect birthday gift for Frances, who would soon turn two.

Her father suggested a spangled ballerina's tutu, but the tiny man shook his head. Tom shook his head repeatedly and gravely that day, until he spotted the Italian puppet theater in a display window. Behind real red-velvet curtains, the stage's hand-painted background was a miniature hearth room with paisley walls and a blazing fire, a veritable model of the sitting room in the apartment below the museum.

Tom chose several handmade finger puppets embroidered with gold thread, including a cat, a bear, and a fish with trailing fins.

He smiled to think of his friend untying the ribbon, shaking the top off the box, of the hot gleam in her almond eyes.

But Frances would never open the package.

Tom watched while Mr. B. slit the envelope. He watched the showman's eyes scan, watched his face collapse and repair itself. If Mr. B. was upset beyond that,

Tom would never know. He waved Tom over, sat him down, and haltingly read the indelicate words on the page (Mrs. B. was not known for her eloquence).

Mr. B. read in an uncharacteristically gentle voice, but as he finished, his eyes wandered. He turned his gold pocket watch, resisting the urge to consult it.

Tom must have looked as stunned as he felt.

Frances had contracted measles, his mentor explained. She had died. Two weeks after they set sail. The letter had taken a month to arrive.

Tom sat like a stone statue — he excelled at it in spite of himself.

"A good and wise Providence has placed her beyond reach of pain or pleasure," Mr. B. said blankly.

It was a thing Tom heard him say often that week, whenever associates offered their sympathy.

Tom crossed his hands in his lap, each thumb trying to overtake the other with alternating success.

He was not consoled.

When Mr. B. demonstrated that he had nothing further to say on the topic, Tom excused himself but felt too weak to climb the stately staircase, a monumental task for one his size. He clambered up on a velvet daybed and curled toward the wall, keeping his shoulders stiff and still, though his upper lip trembled against his wrist.

At Mr. B.'s urging, Ma trudged down and sat by him. She stroked his hair once, but Tom was not consoled.

He curled tighter until his mother went away, murmuring, "Poor Charlie" as she climbed the staircase.

Was it his mother's voice? Tom wasn't sure. It may not have been a real sound at all but a voice from memory or dreams. Either way, the words reminded him of something: he had forgotten his own name.

Tom wept for that lost boy, for the lost girls in the apartment under the great American Museum, for the arrangement of children they would never be again.

Mr. B. could be a wicked prankster or a kind friend, but he was first and always a man of business. If ever Tom's spirits flagged, and they often did that month, Mr. B. knelt, looked him straight in the eye, and squeezed Tom's shoulders for encouragement. "Never is the joke on you, my boy. Remember that. The power is yours. Count your worth in coins." As an afterthought, he added, "Your parents certainly do."

Now that they were a sensation in the court of Queen Vic and Prince Albert, royalty in Europe and beyond clamored for their attention.

You're doing well, my boy.

With so many royal visits, Mr. B. had had a carriage built for Tom, twenty inches high, painted blue and lined with silk, drawn by ponies twenty-eight inches tall and driven by children dressed in livery. The spectacle "killed the public dead," Mr. B. told his associates. Tom was "the greatest hit in the universe."

In Paris, composers wrote songs about him. He starred in a play in which he sprang out of a pie and bounded through the legs of chorus girls. Money poured in. There would always be money.

There would always be applause.

Tom began to wonder if they would ever return home. One year passed and two and finally three.

He wondered, too, did Mr. Barnum never think of his family? Did he never think, as Tom did, of Frances (and Helen)? Mrs. B. and Caroline had sailed over for a visit, but Tom was on another leg of the tour most of that time and rarely saw them.

He received no letters. He sent none.

There was no time.

In the fog of memory, Helen grew achingly real in his thoughts — or less real and more precious. He longed for his fleeting companion but somehow understood that she aligned with Frances, *to* Frances, and was therefore gone for good.

Young as he was, Tom knew that the ladies liked to hold and pet and kiss him. General Tom Thumb was their child, their doll, their merry little man.

Mr. B. took full advantage of the phenomenon.

Tom began selling kisses, twenty-five cents each, along with his autographed biographical booklet. He would one day boast that he had smooched some million fair admirers worldwide.

What Tom didn't say was that until he met the woman he would marry—until he lost his innocence well and truly—his admirers' million faces wore one face. He saw Frances (and Helen), her impish grin in the firelight, and kissed her soundly on the nose.

RETURNING A BLOOM
TO ITS BUD

Those who knew the girl best declared that
she was an industrious, excellent, sensible,
and well-behaved girl . . . altogether too good
for Taylor Barnum.

—P. T. Barnum

The sky was changing. Even she could see that.

Charity retched over the rail again, feeling the first hungry stirrings of the child inside — her fourth.

If you could ignore that sky, or that haze that wasn't sky, the sea ahead was an eerie mirror of the sea behind. She focused on the slicing ship's wake instead. It steadied her, at least until the clank of Caroline's boots on the iron staircase jarred her again. It was an exaggerated stomp worthy of a toddler — something Frances might have done, though no one would have made the mistake of bringing dear, ungovernable Frances on an excursion.

As for Caroline, Charity had tried and failed to settle her in the ladies' salon near the engine room. That suite couldn't be accessed except through the dozen berths reserved for women passengers. The salon had amusements and watchful matrons to spare; it was the safest imaginable place for a twelve-year-old aboard a tin city at sea. But Caroline insisted on returning to their stateroom. She wasn't shy with adult women, but a pair of well-attired twins her own age, traveling with their aunt, were holding court in the common room when they entered. Competitive to a fault, Caroline wouldn't present herself for comparison, even in her new English traveling gown. Not when it was two against one. She skulked back to the hard horsehair bench in the stateroom, and Charity bolted above for fresh air.

Caroline's self-imposed exile had lasted nearly an hour. She emerged now not to check on her sick mother but to break the monotony.

She might be the oldest (the middle Barnum daughter was with her grandmother in Bethel and the youngest, as of February last, in a dark grave), but Caroline had been sulking without a word since her father had deposited them aboard with their trunks, and if she could sulk in public, all the better. "Why did you do it?" she demanded.

"Silent treatment" was Caro's preferred punishment, but all good things come to an end. Charity clutched the rail, waiting for another string of spit to drop from her mouth. How was there anything left to come up? "Do what, darling?"

"Take us away!"

Charity wheeled brightly with a tilt of the head. She would not abide a scene. "And what was your favorite part of the trip, Caroline?"

The girl paused. She was trying to think of a stinger.

How Taylor's voice would ring with approval, Charity remembered, when she stopped him with a joke or a prank or the perfect pointed barb, back in the merry days before they were married. *Chairy gave me a stinger that time, didn't she?*

"The shops," Caroline finally got out. "Until you dragged us away."

There was no consolation like a mother's smile. "I did what was best for you."

"For *me?*"

"You're a very young woman, Caro. England is a wretched nation of drunkards. The very first dinner party we attended, every person drank wine, even the ladies, and I'm sure some of the gentlemen drank a quart apiece."

"But *I* didn't drink wine. So what's the matter?"

There was no place for logic in this struggle. "The poorer classes see this and think they must do the same," Charity said, "but can't afford wine and guzzle ale—"

"We were in France when you decided, not England. France—"

"—is even worse," Charity cut in. Taylor was even now heading back to sample that country's vineyards. "Those half-naked trollops on the stage in Paris ought to be horsewhipped," she said, "and kept on a diet of bread and water."

Charity gave her belly an absent stroke, whether because she was ill—mortally ill, with any luck—or because she was a creature of physical instinct and growing babies had demands. "I can't *wait* to be home again," she gushed. "Ours is the happiest nation in the world, the land of Sabbaths."

"I would *like* to drink wine." Caroline stared past her mother toward the horizon.

Something told Charity there were things happening behind that steel curtain of sky, preparations for a drama that didn't concern her but would make demands anyway.

"I'd like to drink wine from a crystal glass and wear pretty French dresses." Under her breath, Caroline added, "A true French dress would be wasted on *some* people."

Charity had never been pretty. No dress, true or otherwise, would change that, but she was patient. She could forgive rude comments. She could forgive anything, really. Low expectations were her gift to the world. They were how she lived up to her name. (When she was a seamstress in Bethel, back before Taylor proposed to her, people called her Chairy — *rhymes with "fairy"* — a sound like tinkling bells. She was just Charity now. It was the way he introduced her, and Taylor knew everyone before she did.)

"You will return to the stateroom." Dire calm was her one weapon: it hinted at reinforcements outside the frame, adults with more convincing authority, and if that adult be her mother, Caroline's gran, a belt. "I will follow presently."

Caroline crossed her arms in her English dress — green satin with flared sleeves and a flounce, impractical for travel, though who was Charity to say so? At least they'd defected before a French dressmaker could be called in.

The wind was up, just barely, but a surprise swell forced Caroline to uncross her arms and grab a rail. Charity muffled her smile as the wobbly girl marched off.

Mother *wouldn't* follow "presently." It was a white lie. Charity would stay on deck. She would sway and pitch and vomit till the wide salt sea had its fill.

She didn't feel an inkling of the terror now that she had on the trip over—her first-ever transatlantic passage, on the steamer *Great Western*—under a changeless blue sky. On that voyage, her husband and daughter had joined everyone on the ship, it seemed, in teasing and mocking her. Meals in public had been an agony. "Why did you let me come?" Charity had finally burst out at a formal dinner, no longer caring who heard them.

"Now, dear," Taylor soothed, "you know had I objected, you would say it was because I didn't want you."

Across the table, Caroline had nodded sagely: she knew all about it.

Well, Charity *knew*. She had always known. Her husband *didn't* want her.

Taylor might have persuaded her to stay. He might have welcomed her in the first place, invited her out to one of Thumb's royal exhibitions, dressed her up and showed her off at the Egyptian Hall. He *might* have.

Taylor could be generous that way when it suited him.

Instead he had reduced her to shame—an easy feat—suggesting that such amusements, *his* amusements, were beneath her dignity. He wouldn't ban her outright (that was too prudish, against his principles), but he made her the brunt of jokes until she lost the will to defend herself.

He introduced his wife to British colleagues and hangers-on by mortifying her: Charity had moaned piteously the entire voyage, he told all who would listen, terrified the ship would sink and that they would be lost to the "unholy deeps."

As for her seasickness, her husband told gruesome tales designed to turn her stomach another degree. She took *every* remedy, from bicarbonate of soda to powdered charcoal. She had sniffed ammonia, downed water, gallons of it, and subsisted on well-chewed beef, which came up again. She had stuffed cotton in her ears and, removing the cotton to be polite, accepted a commercial remedy in gelatin-capsule form from a fellow passenger.

But increasingly, there was only one medicine that worked, and in a myriad of situations: her doctor was not stingy in prescribing it.

Taylor enjoyed every minute of it—their laughter at her expense. In the privacy of their cabin, he claimed that Charity deserved it. *All that sickly carping.*

Things were no better after they docked. At the hotel in London, Taylor notified her (now that she was too far from home and safety to fuss) that her puling was pathetic; her prejudices were of "quite too long-standing"; she never had anything good to say.

"No," she agreed. "There is nothing good to say about your habits and pastimes."

Card playing, cigar smoking, liquor, and a parade of opera and theater harlots were the least of it, really. Taylor's time alone in Europe with Thumb had been a carnival she was, by her mere presence, intruding upon.

Coming in on the *Great Western* under a cloudless blue sky, Charity had felt a terror larger than any petty cruelty her husband might devise: the light of days might be snatched from her; violence and shipwreck might plunge them into the fathomless deep. These thoughts had obsessed her.

Now, on the way back, the sea did not feel deep enough.

Charity found herself imagining, almost lovingly, the beautiful schools of colored fish, the vivid bars of sunlight, and the secret, scuttling things. For a shameful instant, she even imagined her own white fingers and floating hair, waving like the arms of those anemones Taylor kept in an aquarium case in the American Museum.

She had crossed the Atlantic once. After eight

endless months of vanity and wickedness and the ordeal that was Europe, Charity was only too happy to cross it again. But trapped below deck in the tiny stateroom with her disgruntled child, she felt that her soul was being squeezed to the point of suffocation, and she had to breathe, didn't she? She was with child. Yet another.

Mrs. Barnum would go home, fetch Helen back from Mother, and have at least *one* daughter's sympathy—pity more than sympathy, maybe, but of a quiet sort. And no one would fault her if she didn't hurry back to the apartment under the great crushing clamor of the museum. What if she did more than fetch Helen in Bethel? What if she stayed? Had this baby at her mother's? Taylor would not be home, where he belonged, when the time came. Why should *she* wait there—indefinitely, interminably—for a husband who never arrived and never quite disappeared?

Charity imagined walking with just a carpetbag from the train platform to Bethel, or as far as she could get before her knees buckled or a boot heel snapped. She imagined walking backward in time, growing younger with each step.

"Are you coming?" Caroline was back, at the top of the iron stairwell. "It's time for dinner. They've sounded the gong."

Charity leaned over the rail, poised a moment like a ship's figurehead, but nothing came up. She had lost track of time. The shadows on deck—mast and rigging, deck crew, couples strolling arm in arm—were dark and slanting. The wind had cooled, lifting gooseflesh. There was a new edge to everything.

"I'm *hungry*," Caroline said in her most aggrieved voice.

A stylish lady in a broad hat touched gloved fingers to her throat, facing out to sea to hide her smirk. Gulls wheeled and screamed. Could there be land nearby? Weren't they in the middle of the Atlantic by now? Shouldn't they be? Oh, to end this fitful rocking.

Charity kneaded her handkerchief. They were laughing at her, even without Taylor here to prompt them. She was laughable. If other passengers knew Charity was with child, they would pity or at least tolerate her. But there was no chivalrous knight to clear her path or do her the courtesy of explaining. There was no one to shame the other passengers into decency.

She might have known that marrying into a world of entertainers and moral reprobates—Charity hadn't known, at the time, how big and bright it would all become—would rob her of conventional privileges.

"I'll go without you, then," Caroline pressed on. "The captain will want to make his toast."

"Don't be silly. You can't dine alone. You're not dressed for it."

"Help me, then. I'm *hungry*, Mother."

Charity glanced helplessly at the lady in the hat and her posh gentleman. They were both staring now.

She rested a palm against the V in her bodice and attempted to say *Everyone can hear you* by widening and shifting her eyes. But subtlety was wasted on Caroline; it was not in her nature to be merciful. "I *know* that, Caro. But you can't go in alone. It's unseemly."

"Unseemly?"

"I forbid it. I'll send for supper when I'm well."

"I'm going."

Charity nodded to the nosy couple and caught her daughter by the wrist, drawing her near. "Lower your voice, please," she said into Caroline's hair, enunciating carefully. "You are humiliating yourself."

That deflated her. Caroline resorted to her old standby: "You have no spirit, Mother. *Daddy* would allow it."

"Your father would have you marry a juggler and grow a beard." Charity folded and refolded her handkerchief. "And would not spare you the consequences."

Oh, yes, Taylor was a "good-natured guy," and everyone knew it. He made sure of that. He took things easy. The "old girl," on the other hand, was given to hysterics. Charity looked both ways and leaned close. "There are *men* aboard this ship, Caroline. Lone men, in case you haven't noticed. Not everyone means well."

Her daughter fixed on her the blank eye of innocence. "What are you *talking* about, Mother?"

"Go fetch your shawl," she relented, "and a handbag with a hairbrush. Bring my shawl also."

They would forgo evening wear. Charity was already the laughingstock of the ship. What difference could it make? She was setting a poor example for Caroline, of course, but Charity would lecture her on etiquette once she was well again. There were whole lists of things she would do when she was well again.

Caroline clomped off, and Charity fanned herself with a flared sleeve. She clutched the rail, trying to remember when she had felt this dizzy before. It was no contest, really — Niagara Falls, another disastrous voyage the year before.

That time, Taylor had promised them a real family vacation. Sensible Helen elected to stay behind with Gran, as ever, but Caroline was thrilled and took on adult airs almost from the start. On that trip, for the first but not the last time, she and her father united against Charity. Isolation and despair amplified Charity's symptoms — there were always symptoms, and elixirs, and rest stops.

Her vertigo was so bad on the massive staircase — 250 steps! — leading down to the river that Charity begged to turn back, but Taylor wouldn't have it. "Push on, woman. For once in your life, don't spoil the day for everyone else."

Given to fits of hysteria.

The flow of climbing tourists was relentless. So many bodies, plainly perspiring. Charity couldn't breathe, and when everything began to reel, as now she had grasped the clammy railing and wouldn't let go. Her hand locked on, and even Taylor's firm fingers couldn't pry it loose. He may have tried to move or even lift her. She held firm, a leaden thing.

And so he left her.

Caroline rolled her eyes, and he took his daughter by the arm. They may have glanced back once—Charity couldn't say—and then moved down down down the lurching steps into the cascading press of bodies. The crowd swallowed them, though Charity—through her frozen terror, before she fainted—heard her daughter's mocking voice on the wind: "Daddy! She was so frightened she forgot to be sick!"

Charity remembered little of what came next. She was lifted among gasps and murmurs, conveyed back up the endless staircase by kind gentlemen, strangers—how she blushed to imagine it, their strong hands on and beneath her, all that heaving and grunting.

Later, in Caroline's diary, Charity found only the briefest description of the waterfall: "Sublime," her daughter called it, "as of some misty veil covering beauties unseen to the human eye."

Just now, the hazy veil of the sky above the sea looked different from how it had earlier this afternoon. It had lifted strangely on one side, exposing an amber band of light low on the horizon.

Charity grasped the arm of a passing crewman. "What is that?" She pointed.

He shrugged like a boy caught with his fingers in a pie. "The sky, madam?"

"That light." She regarded him severely, so severely he turned away, heaving his coil of rope higher on one shoulder. It looked heavy, but Charity would and must detain him. "It's a storm, isn't it?"

His eyes spoke what he wouldn't say.

"Will we repair to shore before it comes?"

"No, ma'am. We need the sea room. If we go lee shore, with land downwind, she'll run aground. And besides," he said cavalierly, extending his arms to take in the wide Atlantic, "here we are." The coil of rope slipped to his elbow.

Up above, another sailor shouted from the mast.

"Don't trouble yourself, mum." The man with the rope squeezed her wrist. "We're all seamen here." He walked toward the figure swaying overhead, which was struggling with a British flag that smacked in the wind.

Caroline arrived, draping Charity's shawl over her shoulders from behind, a small kindness: she felt guilty about her insult, the French-dress remark.

Charity gazed at the amber horizon line and the tower of dark-rimmed clouds bunching above it. If they were to be swept into the sea, let her be the woman and mother she was meant to be. *As of some misty veil covering beauties unseen to the human eye.* Let her be quiet.

* * *

Perhaps she was too frightened to be sick, but tonight the smells of oxtail broth and boiled cabbage didn't provoke her. Charity sat passing the butter and the chutney. She smiled faintly at fellow passengers in their proper dinner dress. She laughed at the captain's merry jokes and pretended not to notice when daylight was snuffed out, much too early, as if between the fingers of a giant. The oily darkness that came on was so sudden, it reminded her of when the museum's Drummond light was turned off in the wee hours and stopped streaking past their bedroom window.

"Steering way means the ship is proceeding with enough power to steer," a spectacled man across the table told his business companion. "Rather than just getting jostled by waves and wind." Charity knew from breakfast that the man had served in the British navy.

"To plow through safely," he went on, "the ship must keep its bow pointing into the waves, or a big one striking the side could roll the vessel and sink it."

His companion patted his breast pocket, in need of tobacco, but the veteran wouldn't stop.

"Wind and waves will try to turn a vessel." The navy man pursed his lips and nodded, as if agreeing with another speaker. "To push against them begs forward momentum."

His friend now looked quite pale, and the captain brought a scolding finger to his lips. "Ladies," he said with that rugged charm peculiar to ships' captains, "you'll have noticed a slight turn in the weather. But sleep soundly this night if you please." He stood and bowed, setting down his napkin. "Things are well in hand."

The party, their faces desperate, watched him go. Caroline was too intent on the beautiful twin gowns at the next table to notice — the sisters from the salon. Charity found their laughter alarming in the hush. Most everyone else seemed to be listening for something on the wind.

She focused on the elegant room, with its proud columns of white and gold, its decor in soft hues of lemon and blue. Waiters trod Oriental carpets, bustling through arched doorways. Dozens of gilded wall mirrors gave the illusion of space, reflecting sparkling glassware and ladies' jewels. The soft hiss of gas lamps was oddly comforting.

But at this point, the ship that had seemed so massive docked in Liverpool was, to her mind, a toy boat in the monstrous grasp of the sea.

What Charity hadn't noticed until now was that all the tasteful furniture was bolted down.

After much nervous laughter and hand shaking, the dinner crowd dispersed.

In their berth, Charity sat on the lower of two narrow bunks, fully clothed apart from the shawl she had forgotten on the back of her dining-room chair. They might be evacuated, after all. They might have to leap into lifeboats. That was the truth, and it paralyzed Charity: there was no other truth now but the sea.

"Aren't you going to put on your nightcap?" Caroline climbed to the top bunk in crisp new French linens. She'd wriggled out of her corset the moment they retired, and normally Charity would, too.

Instead, she ignored the doctor's dropper and took a swig of tincture straight from the bottle to calm her nerves. The wind was a howling beast, but were not wolves more terrifying at a distance? Wasn't it worse to hear them approaching? When you weren't yet resigned?

Let it come, she thought.

Not the storm, of course. The floating. The down-downdeep into dreamless sleep of her favorite remedy. Next she knew, the air was the color of smoke from damp fuel. She could taste it, but she was blind. She was *all ears* (such a funny phrase). Was she awake and remembering? Or asleep and dreaming? Here? Or there? It didn't matter. The steely sounds of gusting rain and distant thunder were in both places — both times — background.

The day she and Taylor met, there hadn't been a cloud in the sky when Charity rode out to fetch her bonnet at the milliner's.

Grassy Plain was just a mile northwest of where

she boarded and worked in Bethel, but during her exchange with the hatmaker, rain began to batter the roof. The room grew so dark that Miss Wheeler went around and lit the candles. *The air was the color of smoke from damp fuel.* Charity had to decline her host's offer to stay the night—she had obligations—so the milliner sent her assistant across to alert Mrs. Rushia. A young clerk in her store rode to Bethel every Saturday to visit his mother. The mud tonight would be treacherous. Might the two ride in together?

He was a jovial young fellow, Miss Wheeler assured her.

Charity knew the names Taylor *and* Barnum, of course; they were old family lines in the region. But she couldn't place this native son in her thoughts.

What she felt when his frame filled the milliner's doorway and her pulse filled her ears was pain, exquisite, dark pain. That a man, any man—much less the swaggering young specimen with curling hair and cleft chin that walked in—should attend her, pretending at chivalry in the candles' glow (even as his eye strayed past her to something beyond, some alternative present only he could see), was inconceivable.

But the danger passed. Young Barnum turned out to be polite and gracious, handing her up to her saddle, withdrawing his hand from her gloved one not a moment too late.

They trotted toward Bethel side by side, and Charity

couldn't recall now what they talked about that night on the road, only that it felt easy and natural, that she had laughed loudly and often. He later told her he had regretted that it was only a mile to town. "When that bolt of lightning—you remember it," he said, "we both jumped in the saddle—gave me a fair view of your face, I wished for twenty more miles."

He had helped her down at her door and offered to settle her horse in the barn, bowing as they parted ways. "Miss Charity."

"Mr. Taylor," she replied with a half smile, and it dawned on her as she walked inside that she hadn't even blushed, saying his name.

Maybe he would be the one, she thought that night in bed. He would draw her out, coax her from the tight bud of awkwardness that doomed her, at best, to a small and ordinary life. Charity would bloom not for him but because of him, and perhaps his faults, whatever they might be, would not matter then. There was no returning a bloom to its bud.

She woke to a dismal shriek.

Caroline was dangling from above, flailing her arms and thumping on the underside of her bunk, trying to wake her mother. Charity sat bolt upright, balancing with one hand on the wall and the other gripping the edge of her thin mattress. She heard shouts and weeping in the halls, a clamor of footfalls on deck. There was an electric crackle out there and great shifting and clanking noises in the ship's belly. The room pitched and tilted wildly, strangely illuminated, though it was still night. By lightning? The moon? Charity saw a faint sparkle where the carpet should be — water sloshing all around, with objects bobbing in it.

"I tried to wake you!" Caroline sobbed. Her voice was hoarse and her hand hung limply. "I tried, but you wouldn't wake. You wouldn't ..."

"Find something to hold on to up there," Charity shouted. "Don't lean that way! You'll tumble off...."

Caroline rolled out of view, no doubt relieved to have a witness at last. How alone she must have felt! Charity winced at the thought. "Don't be afraid," she offered in a thin voice, and the hilarity of the words struck her. Beside her bed, the water pitcher plunged and bobbed like a porpoise. Everything loose among their belongings was afloat.

She couldn't help it. She began to giggle.

"Are you *laughing?*" Caroline accused, dangling again. "Have you gone mad?"

"You look very pretty upside down," Charity said, and now they both giggled, or Caroline snorted to keep from giggling.

Just when it seemed the ship would roll over completely, it creaked and lurched back the other way. Sometimes it seemed the stateroom was standing on end, and Charity balanced in her nook by fitting her feet here or there against the wall or the metal fittings of the bunk. Her knuckles on the rail were the color of new cream.

The ship heaved back the other way, slowly, with a sickening grace. A slap of salt spray doused them.

This violent dance went on for perhaps an hour, diminishing by tiny degrees. Wet and shivering, Charity folded around the baby like petals closed tight. She let the conviction bloom inside her: this was not the end.

When it was safe to stand, Charity grasped the metal rail spanning the room. Most of the water had seeped out, but the floor was slick. Her heels skidded, and her muscles seized, sending a sharp pain through her back, but she braced herself and made it to the porthole.

The retreating clouds were piled high, illuminated by scattered lightning. The flashes exposed visible sheets of rain. It was profoundly beautiful. Charity moved her hand from the small of her back to her belly. She breathed a sigh and clutched the rail again, circling back to the bunk. She climbed the ladder and collapsed beside Caroline, who hugged her furiously.

"I'm here," she told her firstborn. "I'm here." Charity sang tunelessly into her daughter's damp hair. "*'Blacks and bays, dapples and grays . . . All the pretty little horses.'*"

She remembered how baby Frances would whimper in the night—often around the time the Drummond light at the top of the American Museum blinked out, committing the city to night — almost as if she knew she wouldn't stay long.

Charity listened, and they were one heartbeat: she and Caroline and the baby who wasn't yet, and the baby who no longer was, and the girl at home with her grandmother, asleep with a pet mouse under her blanket.

"'When you wake, you'll have cake, and all the pretty little horses.'"

Morning would be like the first morning, washed clean, everyone aboard ship smiling and trading tales of peril and surrender, their steps squishing in the Oriental carpets as the captain raised a toast at breakfast.

The night Chairy and Taylor rode home drenched to the skin, she had laughed more than she ever would again. She had felt reckless — exposed, along with her curves in wet clothes — like a girl in a gothic story, not a demure seamstress with broken buttons on her boot.

It was her laughter along with her "stout assets" and "beautiful white teeth," he said, that bewitched him that night on the stormy road from Grassy Plain to Bethel. Whenever their paths crossed after that, Taylor bartered for her laughter the way he did his customers' money behind the shop counter, with great energy and pride. And little by little, her stores decreased. And what profit he earned, he quickly spent.

Where would he go next? she wondered. After

France and its vineyards? Charity hadn't asked. She had learned early that she had no claims on her husband's outsize ambition. There had been the one night, during a storm like this one, when she felt beautiful, blessed with something more than an ordinary fate — but the facts had proved otherwise, and she is not Niagara, not a thundering, racing thing. Not made of big passions. What innocent passions do surge up, Charity drowns like kittens, for she has no use for them, no room.

BESIDE MYSELF

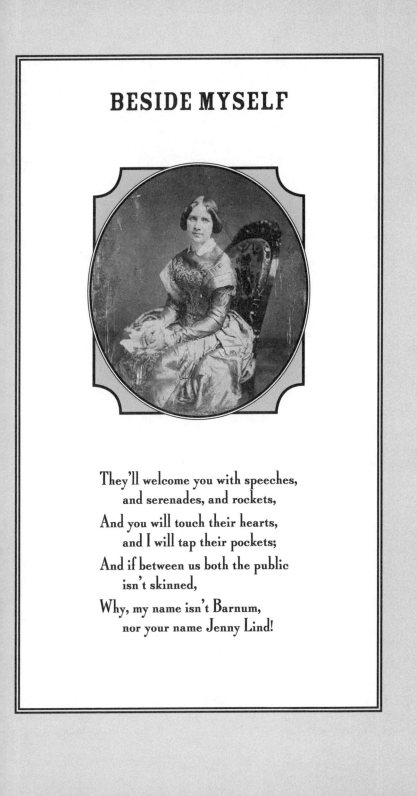

They'll welcome you with speeches,
    and serenades, and rockets,

And you will touch their hearts,
    and I will tap their pockets;

And if between us both the public
    isn't skinned,

Why, my name isn't Barnum,
    nor your name Jenny Lind!

Jo heard the chanting long before the river-
boat chugged up to the First Municipality. The
moment the *Falcon* bumped the dock, the swarm
of bodies below became animated—a swirl of colored
silks, parasols, and flags, hundreds and hundreds—just
as they had at wharves and stations all over the East
Coast.

Behind the curtained window, Jo felt the now-
familiar panic. She had survived it so far by telling herself stories when she waited: today she was Andromeda
from the Greek myths, chained to a cliff, about to be
sacrificed to the sea monster. Fame (it wasn't even *hers*!)
was a monstrous thing, in Jo's experience, and there was
no hero, no Perseus, here to rescue her.

The police kept the gangway barred while customs
officials finished their work, and soon Mr. Barnum
returned with his report: everything was set. As crowds
went, this was a good-natured one, relaxed and cheerful.

"Ready?" He looked at Jo.

The dining room had emptied. Most passengers had
filed out or lost interest in the rumor that P. T. Barnum
and a famous opera singer were aboard, departing in
New Orleans. They had trickled back to their berths.
Only Jenny's entourage stood by.

Jo nodded demurely. She *wasn't* ready. She never
would be. The blood beat so hard in her ears it drowned

out the patter of practical encouragement that attended every landing. She hoped there were no new instructions, because she wouldn't hear them. Jo was in the sea monster's shadow.

At the showman's nod, Mr. Blakely stepped forward and crooked an arm, his eyes begging her pardon. Everyone knew how she felt about this routine, how it pained her—Jenny more than anyone, and Jo was finding it increasingly difficult to forgive her for that.

She brushed the green veil over her face, linked an arm though Blakely's, and stepped out into the swampy air. Jo moved down the gangway in graceful unison with her escort, just as Jenny had taught her to, shielding her eyes less against the glare than the prying eyes of strangers.

It was Jenny Lind, the Swedish Nightingale, they were here for. It was Jenny they chanted for. But it was rarely Jenny they got, at least offstage. Mr. Barnum had devised decoys to spare his star's nerves, and what Jenny needed, Jenny would have.

So it had always been. So it would always *be*.

Jo was too startled to react when a man elbowed his way through the crowd and charged the gangway, shouting. If not for Mr. Blakely, who shielded her with his person, easing Jo back up the creaking planks, she could have been mowed down or knocked into the water. Two officers caught the intruder (he went limp in their grip like a dog pulled from a fight, as if he didn't know what had come over him).

Mr. Blakely kept a hand on the small of her back while they retreated aft, a too-familiar gesture ordinarily, an insult to a gentlewoman, but under the circumstances it felt fatherly and protective.

Jenny had seen it all from behind the curtain in the dining room. She rushed out to fold Jo into her arms and then tried to lift her veil and meet her eyes. Jo turned, holding the veil flat, a shield. She would not be seen or pitied.

Her friend seemed to think it was fine, sending her out disguised as Jenny Lind, putting her pet Josephine on display (not to mention in danger), but it wasn't fine. Not with Jo. No one had thought to ask her. It had become a part of her job description at some point, that was all, and when Jo thought to protest, the words died on her tongue. She was too proud. This was so obviously wrong, and Jenny overlooked it, which spoke for itself. As Jo had told her mother in a letter, the trouble with being a lady's traveling companion was that the lady made the itinerary.

"Poor delicate girl." Jenny glanced back at the gathering crowd on deck, stroking the silk where Jo's cheek would be. "*Dear* Jo."

Jo did something surprising then. She pushed past the Nightingale, past the gawping Miss Barnum in her identical green veil (the showman's daughter was understudy to the understudy, and up next), past the contrite Mr. Blakely, still pink with exertion.

She retreated to her narrow berth upstairs, leaving the others to regroup. The party's trunks were already on deck, awaiting porters. The narrow bed had been stripped bare. But the cabin door was still unlocked, and Jo closed herself in. She let down her veil like a penitent, smoothing the salt tracks from her cheeks.

She heard one of Barnum's men on deck bark, "Make way for Mr. Barnum and Miss Lind!" followed by a roar of excitement. There would be more policemen, reinforcements below the gangway now, and Jo knew what would happen next. It had all been staged, blocked out at breakfast. But she no longer needed to "rehearse": she had been through the ordeal before. Far too many times.

The crowd—everyone from elegant Creole belles to rough-bearded Californians—would murmur and part agreeably. But when officers led the pair across the teeming levee to the carriage, they'd be mobbed all over again. The police would spread their arms and shield them, and once the two were finally seated, once the horses clopped off with the carriage, the whole witless crowd would move with it, as mythical krakens moved with the tide.

Jo had seen the etchings. New Orleans was full of balconies. There would be ladies waving handkerchiefs from above as Barnum and his fake bird bounced past.

The carriage would advance by slow degrees, painfully slowly, with all those people circling it on foot, some pressing their hands and faces to the carriage windows. Mr. Barnum never closed the shades, even for the real Jenny. He would smile and wave and expect his star (or her double) to do the same.

Jenny was scheduled to leave next — quietly, of course, and incognito. But she stopped by Jo's door first, rapping on the wood with her knuckles like a man. "Jo-bird?"

Jo liked to think that Jenny was concerned, afraid even. Was this the last straw? Would Jo go away before Otto arrived to replace her, leaving the Nightingale to survive her own company? "We'll talk later," Jo murmured through the wood. "Go or you'll be crushed."

The truth was, there was nothing to say. There were a great many things to say, but Jo no longer trusted herself to say them. She had to stay focused. Plans like this were easy for the others. Belletti and the orchestra had no cause for worry; they had been sent ahead and were already settled in their lodgings. Not so for Jo. When something urgent was expected of her, the panic could literally take her breath away. Jo would race to find a water closet and clutch her throat, believing . . . *knowing* . . . she would die.

She knew the captain would be holding a carpetbag with a change of outerwear for her. Jo would slip on the drab new cloak and veil. Barnum always included a yellow parasol, too, should one of his Jennys need to be found in a surging crowd.

She would take the arm of another escort from their group, a man whose role was to *in no way* resemble Mr. Barnum or anyone else (the showman had called Mr. Archer "nondescript" to his face while they were strategizing that morning, which struck Jo as cruel), and the party would convene at the night's lodgings.

So it went.

Next to no one was left on the levee to notice when she and Mr. Archer stepped into the hackney cab parked discreetly by the curb.

They had pulled it off again, what Mr. Barnum called "diva doubling." How he enjoyed his games! No man was better matched to his profession, Jo thought, smiling wearily at Mr. Archer.

She laid her head back against the cushion and closed her eyes, enjoying the quiet. In the carriage a few blocks ahead of them, the Nightingale would likely be frowning. Jenny would be deep in that commanding fog of her own design that protected her and made her hard and cold when she had to be. Her critics complained of her "Nordic reserve," but the ice was all Jenny's.

Of even more interest at the moment was Caroline Barnum, no doubt stalled in *her* carriage a few blocks ahead of Jenny's. How did it feel to be a young American woman (with few talents or prospects beyond her father's money) surrounded by maniacal fans? How was it for Caroline Barnum to be — and also *not* be — Jenny Lind for a day?

Jo meant to speak to Miss Barnum in private about the phenomenon of playing Jenny. It was one thing to pose as someone else, behind a veil, and another to pose as a *specific* someone (not a "type," as at a masked ball, where you posed as a "queen" or a "Gypsy"), and in Jo's case a person you knew intimately. To masquerade as one of your oldest childhood friends felt intrusive (different than reading Jenny's letters or journal, and in fits of fury and rebellion, Jo had read both). By this point in their friendship, in the tour, she could *almost* hear Jenny's thoughts. She could guess how her friend might respond in this or that situation. She could, in other words, do more than masquerade (it was a pity Jo couldn't sing). But she didn't wish to. Of Jenny's conquests, only Otto concerned her — but better not to think about that.

She had no right to think about him.

As for Miss Barnum, who seemed to revel in pretending to be the Nightingale, Jo had it on good authority that Jenny would trade it all tomorrow, if she could, for freedom and anonymity. She would be someone else if she could. The other morning in Cuba Jenny had described a dream in which she stepped out of her body and let it drop to the floor in a heap like a discarded gown (or a sealskin from the old tales). At the pinnacle of her professional life, Jenny was plotting her escape from opera—from stardom—and she would marry to do it if she had to. She would marry Otto.

Because she could.

When Mr. Archer began to snore on the bench across from her, Jo opened her eyes and craned to see Jenny's carriage ahead, but there was no sign of it.

Here they were again, two plain brown birds, except that eluding notice was an ordinary day for Jo, while all of America knew Jenny. She belonged to them. Barnum had made certain of that long before they arrived from Europe. Her likeness was everywhere—if much idealized, Jo thought. Jenny was no beauty—everyone remarked on it. When you saw her on the street, you wouldn't think she could inspire devotion or fervor. But then she opened her mouth.

Jo imagined their three carriages as if inked on a map, traveling separate routes but converging in Jackson Square, and eventually they did.

Their driver steered the horses to the curb by a lavish brick apartment block that curved around a corner of the square. He got in line with the other carriages, and Barnum, in the first of the three, climbed out to a great cheer.

As he took Caroline's hand and helped her down, the roar was deafening, and as Miss Barnum removed her veil with a flourish (and a wry smile), there was a huge collective sigh, a release of laughter. "That's not her!" someone barked into a cupped hand, and heads began to swivel. "Where have you hidden her, Barnum?"

"Barnum! Barnum!"

The chant soon flipped as Mr. Archer stepped out of the third carriage. Public attention wheeled to them, and though Jo's heart hammered, she knew she would soon be indoors and "off duty," as it were. She took his upstretched hand, lifted her hem, and stepped down.

"Jenny Lind! Jenny Lind!"

Jo dropped her veil to quiet them, fixing her eyes on the cobblestones as Mr. Archer steered her through the police barricade while the good-natured crowd murmured and laughed. They had been duped again. They took it well, nodding and lifting hats and caps, bowing as she passed.

Jo climbed the steps to the Pontalba building after the Barnums, and, as planned, each Jenny paused at the ornate iron railing to wave (bow, in Miss Barnum's case, an improvisation) for applause before ducking into the foyer.

Jenny's escort helped her down from the middle carriage. She removed her veil with a grateful bow, pivoting to take in teeming Jackson Square, and her admirers applauded as thunderously as if she had just delivered the *romanza* from *Robert le Diable*, hooting and stomping and waving bouquets and banners.

"Jenny Lind O! Jenny Lind O!"

Safe in the hall, Jo could afford to smile at her friend's composure as Jenny joined their waiting circle.

It had all been choreographed, every bit of it— right down to the bullish man on the gangway, she supposed.

She couldn't remember how she reached the door of the suite. Things blurred that way, in the moment, but their hostess, the Baroness Pontalba—who had loaned her lavish apartments for the occasion—sent a maid away with their wraps and walked both Jennys to a half-circle of satin chairs.

The suite was already full to bursting, with the air of a party. Uniformed staff buzzed around with canapés and drinks, and until Jenny was admitted, visitors held court around Barnum and the heavily made-up baroness, who stopped talking only long enough to greet Jenny and walk her—so plain and petite—over to the chair beside Jo.

Jenny smoothed her gown and nodded, her face set between contrition and arrogance, and Jo hoped she would at least pretend not to be bored with the fuss.

The baroness listened raptly to Barnum's account of the trip from the wharf. Their entourage of hundreds had walked the entire route with their transport, he said, crowding round in a cacophony of whistles, chants, brass, and woodwinds—there had been a tuba stationed very near her window, Miss Barnum put in, beaming—bumping and jostling along with the carriage. It was a wonder the city hadn't completely shut down.

"I don't see how you bear it." The baroness glanced from Barnum to Jenny, who looked comfortable, at least, in her low satin chair. "Such an entitled crowd is like gunpowder, yes? And about as brainless."

Mr. Barnum was in his element. "On the contrary, Baroness. The public *enjoys* being deceived, *delights* in it so long as they're amused." And it was his job to make certain they were. "In London we took them in most deliciously, didn't we, Caro?" He turned to his daughter, who lit up. "Tell them about Thumb."

Shyly at first, and then with energy, the showman's daughter leaned forward and told how she had relayed the tiny general—swaddled like a baby—through a crowd as large as the one gathered outside. "His mother usually carried him, but I took over once when she was tired. The crowd never thought twice!"

Jo smiled. The showman's daughter enjoyed the game as much as her father did. Miss Barnum found the fun in it. She even seemed to covet the role, and Jo would be only too happy to hand it over entirely, but convincing Jenny was another matter. It was hard enough, the Nightingale insisted, to maintain her dignity as an artist during this American circus. *Let's not add insult to injury.*

"You must tell them about Baltimore," Jo said to Miss Barnum, though Jenny wouldn't like it. Jenny *didn't* like it: Jo could tell by the look in her eye.

But innocent Caroline told the tale with relish. Congregants at a Baltimore church who had glimpsed her with her father the day before mistook Miss Barnum for the opera star.

"My songbird joined her local friend in the choir, and the congregation swooned," her father put in, giving Caroline's shoulder a nudge. "'Heavenly!' the papers said of her decidedly . . . average voice. 'Exquisite!'"

The assembly had a good laugh, and the daughter was unfazed by her father's teasing, but Jenny's expression darkened.

The real Nightingale had tried and failed to be jovial at the time. "Promiscuous crowds," she'd complained to Jo in private, bitterly. How could she trust her talent to them? Her years of training? Her "genius," if that word be bandied about, when their ardor came so cheap? When all it took was a bit of coin and a brilliant huckster to bedazzle them?

Whatever Jenny might think, Miss Barnum was a gift to Jo, who praised her impersonation skills and fed her ambition every chance she got.

To appease the stubborn crowd — those from the levee and hundreds more now clustered outside the building, chanting for Jenny and for Barnum — Madame

Pontalba stepped onto the balcony to cheers and laughter. She began a lively banter with folks in the crowd, but their chant built like a bonfire.

"Jenny Lind O! Jenny Lind O!
Come to the window."

"I don't think we can hold off your southern admirers much longer," Mr. Barnum urged Jenny gently (he had learned restraint in their weeks together on tour; Jenny had trained him, as she did all the important men in her life, to check his enthusiasms), turning back from the window. "They won't be satisfied," he said, "until you step out and wave."

"They won't be satisfied at all." Jenny's priceless voice had a flat edge, and the baroness stepped in, extending a heavily ringed hand. When Jenny didn't take it, she said, "You are tired, dear?"

Jenny knew her duty, but she could be stubborn.

"Come to the window.... Come to the window...."

Jo leaned over and took Jenny's hand. "You'll get to your bed sooner if you say good night."

Jenny rose abruptly, all the eyes in the room rising with her, and strode past the baroness and out onto the balcony. "Thank you, my friends!" She waved her handkerchief, head erect, and her presence surged through them. "See you tomorrow night?"

Even from inside, Jo heard the murmur of collective

approval. Jenny drew back, still waving. "Good night!"

She went inside and pulled the balcony doors closed. At once, the chanting dropped off, and she took her seat again.

The room was hot and hushed. Jenny's mood had infected them all. Her preparations had been made. The star's every need had been anticipated and attended to, her gowns and capes brushed and hung, her local staff interviewed and dispatched, and the merriment was over before it had begun, though the pleasantries wore on.

During one of the baroness's self-involved stories, Jo walked back to the lavish bedchamber to see that Jenny's one precious object, a locked box of letters — mostly personal correspondence from Felix, with yellowing scraps of his music — had been set out on the vanity beside her mother's bone hairbrush. Jenny didn't bother to keep Otto's letters in that box. They were everywhere, strewn about for Jo to find and read in secret, wincing word by word.

When she came back, Jo unlaced Jenny's boots and pushed over an ottoman for her to prop her feet on. "Tea with honey?" This homey activity signaled an end to the evening.

Jenny shook her head, turning her cheek to rest it against the satin.

The baroness rallied. "Well, then," she said to all stragglers, smiling at Barnum. "We should let you rest. It's a pleasure to have you, and I hope my humble rooms offer comfort far from home."

There was gratitude and murmuring, though there was nothing humble about either the baroness or her apartments. When the party left, she would sell at auction every single object Jenny Lind had touched.

"Lindomania" had greeted them at every port since New York, and by opening night there would be Jenny Lind bonnets, shawls, gloves, opera vests, and ties for purchase. Around the nation, pianos, perfume, pancakes, ceramic busts, cigars, and singing teakettles were for sale in Jenny's name. Rumor had it there was even a butcher here in New Orleans, at the Poydras Market, selling Jenny Lind sausages, five for a picayune.

Jenny—and the charities her work supported—would see no profit from any of this.

Barnum joined the bustle to clear the room, and Jo heard him whisper to Caroline to stand by. Dinner was en route. "She wants you to stay and dine with them. To thank you."

Caroline Barnum looked alarmed, but Jo stood and squeezed her wrist for encouragement. (She hoped to excuse herself after dinner. A guest improved her chances of getting away without a scene. Jenny sometimes couldn't sleep, and Jo needed to.)

Mr. Barnum extracted the last of the stragglers in his jovial way and then let himself out. The three women sat awkwardly for a time. Miss Barnum even (absurdly) got up and tried to help the maid distribute their meal until Jenny asked her to stop. "Please sit, Miss Barnum. You are our guest. Our hero, if you will. Isn't that so, Josephine?" She looked from Miss Barnum to Jo and sighed expansively. "My trusty other selves."

The showman's daughter looked bravely from one to the other. "Please," she said, "call me Caroline."

They started in on the oyster stew the maid had ladled into their bowls. Caroline's eyes roamed the roomful of glorious antiques. She either refused to look at Jenny or couldn't bring herself to and was so nervous that Jo might have felt sorry for her if she weren't so busy feeling sorry for herself.

The stew was delicious. Madame Pontalba had summoned the famous chef Boutdro from Paris for Jenny's stay, but it was a waste. Jo could have told her that. Jenny craved only herring and potatoes. She wanted a clean wooden chair, she said, and a wooden spoon to eat milk soup with. She longed for a home that wasn't, it seemed, some nostalgic or idealized version of their lives in Sweden, before she became celebrated. The same life Jo would go on living when she went home, except when Jenny—who had had no home growing up, she claimed, except in leaving it; she had learned to keep house in her head—pulled Jo along like a toy elephant on a string for comfort.

But if Jenny was a bird in a very gilded cage, she had chosen it. Jo had not. Not really.

Jo had consented to travel as Jenny's formal "companion." They had been friends since school, so Jo might have gone anyway, but the salary was generous and helped justify leaving Mamma, who was unwell. ("Don't speak to me of mothers," Jenny had spat, as if her tragic history trumped all, and didn't it? Mustn't it?) But as the tour wore on, Jo came to feel imprisoned and resentful. Her job was undefined. The work was whatever Jenny wanted on any given day, in any given moment, too much for Jo or anyone (*Poor Otto*, Jo thought daily — *poor, poor love*), and if Jenny felt you slipping away, beyond her charms and endearments, her refuge was tyranny.

Jo had never wanted a thing so much as she wanted this tour to end. But she couldn't leave Jenny now, here, in this strange, loud universe of Barnum.

When they had finished their crème brûlée and drained their teacups, Jo asked to turn in. *Haven't I suffered enough today?* her eyes commanded.

"I have a touch of headache," she tried, though Jenny looked up sharply.

The Nightingale's silence was her answer.

Jenny had a headache of her own, no doubt, three times the size of Jo's, an *important* headache, and still managed to be gracious. "You must have been frightened today, Jo," she offered instead. "That terrible man."

"He really did come out of nowhere," Caroline agreed. She might have been as cowed by Jenny as any fan off the street, but as Barnum's daughter, she understood spectacle. She knew that fame was, at least in part, manufactured.

"That time in Baltimore," Jenny began—it surprised Jo that she would return to the subject—"I remember standing on a balcony like this one." Jenny gestured toward the double doors. "It was the same day you outsang me, I think." She looked at Caroline, who blushed fiercely, but Jo could see it pleased her. Miss Barnum was not the wilting violet she seemed to be. "I accidentally let my shawl slip from my shoulders," Jenny said, "and the crowd seized it like some saint's garment in a medieval market." She looked from one dinner companion to the other, her eyes glazed. She was tired, Jo knew, too tired to sleep, to rest her nerves. "They ripped it to shreds for souvenirs."

Jo reached out and took Jenny's hand (it wasn't in her job description, no, but it might have been—it was what made her indispensable, this gift for consoling).

"It won't surprise Jo," Jenny said, "that I was a pious, troubled child, fascinated with saints and martyrs."

Jo smiled on cue. Jenny had told this story a great many times, at a great many tables, from Milan to Moscow.

It was all new to Caroline, who took it in like a child waiting for the end of a bedtime story.

"As a young touring musician, I sometimes imagined I was Saint Catherine of Sweden, besieged by dissolute young lords who would seduce the virgin on her pilgrimage. A provident God, of course, would thwart them." Jenny laughed, and so did Jo, dutifully. "And perhaps the real point of the game was to replace my own scolding mother with Catherine's. Birgitta was a saint, too," she explained, "and their bond was tender, heaven-sent."

It would be hours, Jo saw, hours and hours, before Jenny would be able to sleep, before *they* would be able to sleep. She would hold them captive as long as she could. Jo's mind drifted as Jenny regaled Caroline — fresh blood, a rapt audience: the Barnum apartment was just downstairs, so Jenny was happy to detain the young woman, and Jo, well, Jo didn't matter — with tales of touring Europe as an opera star.

"There were saints everywhere," she said. "Real ones in plain view, their relics enshrined in all the old churches: they were clots of blood in vials, curls of cured skin, chips of bone, limbs in gilded boxes. Once, I saw a figgy heart framed with pearls." Jenny liked that phrase especially well, Jo knew from past dinner banter, past tour stops. She never failed to use the word *figgy*.

"Another time, a whole mummified corpse dressed in lace and satin." She looked up gleefully. "Encased just like the curiosities in your father's museum."

"What made a mob hungry for blessings worship a fingernail?" Jenny mused aloud, not expecting, or wanting, an answer. Hadn't Orpheus, the musician of ancient

Greece, been ripped to shreds by maenads frenzied by his song?

Can I go to bed now?

At some point in the evening, even Jenny seemed to run out of things to say. The room was unbearably hot, so Jo stood to open the balcony doors again. Remarkably, there was still a crowd of revelers out there, and the chanting flared up again, faint and provisional.

"Jenny Lind O! Jenny Lind O! . . . window . . . Lind O!"

Did they think she would come back out? Or was her visit just an excuse for merriment (not that you needed one, Jo supposed, in New Orleans)?

The view of Jackson Square from the balcony — St. Louis Cathedral, the court buildings, the wide Mississippi beyond — would bring solace at sunrise, she knew, before the streets swarmed with tourists and curiosity seekers. Jo froze a moment, uncertain what to do now that she had opened Pandora's box. She let the doors drift not completely closed and stepped back.

Caroline thanked them both, tidied a bit, and excused herself gracefully. They hardly heard her leave, but Jo could imagine her reeling thoughts. Like many larger-than-life people, Jenny had a way of roping you in only to withdraw again, revoking all intimacy or privilege. It was her prerogative. Everyone who traveled with her knew it, but Caroline was only attached to a small portion of the tour, and she was young.

* * *

Opening days were Jo's favorite, when Jenny and Belletti were rehearsing with the orchestra, sequestered at the theater.

It rained perpetually in this city, or the humidity always made rain seem imminent, and she was on the steps of the apartment building, deciding whether to bring a parasol, when Caroline found her. She must have seen that Jo was adrift. Jo mumbled something about stepping out for a quiet cup of tea. She thought she would sit a while in the lobby of a nearby hotel that Madame Pontalba had recommended and answer letters.

"I'll walk you there," Caroline said.

Instead of feeling intruded upon or disappointed, Jo was surprised at her relief. Caroline took control of the morning in a way that suited her, and within minutes of their walk, the two Jennys were laughing and confiding in each other.

"Confess," Caroline demanded shamelessly. "Are all the men in love with her?"

"Oh, yes. I could tell you a thing or two."

"Tell! Tell!"

"Oh, I can't," Jo objected, but she did.

It came gushing out.

She told Caroline about Jenny's many suitors, famous men like the writer Hans Christian Andersen, who had written the Nightingale into his fairy tales and who pined after her for years. She told of Jenny's two broken engagements and Chopin's deathbed and the tragedy of Felix, Jenny's great love, who was married when they met and died under mysterious circumstances, perhaps at his own hand, breaking his muse's heart forever. "Belletti's in love with her, too," she whispered when they paused before a shop window. "Benedict told her he swoons all night, and now she has to keep him at arm's length and still manage to sing with him. It's madness."

Caroline could only shake her head.

"Even now she's weighing a marriage suit," Jo said, with more sadness in her voice than she intended. "An old friend."

Jo did not tell who that friend was. She could not speak his name, and besides it was the dullest of tales — and all the more piercing and precious for it. In her secret heart, Jo believed that Otto was too good for Jenny precisely *because* he was simple and ordinary, modest and kind — however gifted he might be as a musician and composer.

He had written again asking only after Jenny's welfare, asking again, Could he be of service to her? Could he ease her difficulties in any way? Become her foremost supporter in all ways? Otto saying without saying what he had claimed all along, that he was her truest and most devoted friend.

He was consistent that way, and he was right.

And in her defense, Jenny was taking his suit seriously. Did she want a home only to run away from it? Could she make him happy? She was asking all the right questions. Fickle will not do, Jo had counseled her, keeping her voice steady when it touched his name. *You could have anyone.* Not for Otto. "He doesn't deserve so little. You must be sure." *Anyone at all.*

A cluster of people standing by the cathedral noticed them and began to point. "They must have seen us yesterday," Caroline said, linking her arm through Jo's and steering them in the opposite direction. "Word this morning was that people are spilling off the early ferries. The merchants are all setting out tables."

The fashionable thoroughfares of the city were already alive as if for a festival. On Chartres Street, all the shop doors were open. Jo heard a merchant stacking bolts of beautiful fabric shout across to jeweler, "I'll have a Jenny Lind in town every winter!"

There were so many people out milling, strolling, browsing, buying, that Jo felt a blush of pride. Jenny was certainly good for business.

As they approached the St. Charles Theatre (and Jenny's name in lights), Jo saw men breathing fire and wrestling mammoth hogs in pens. The open lots near the building were full of peddlers crying their wares:

oysters and crayfish and pralines. A man poked a drooling grizzly bear in a cage with a stick to separate it from the rabble of boys jostling to touch its fur. Jo hid her face against Caroline's shoulder as they passed, pitying the exhausted animal.

Caroline was worldly in her way and pointed out at least one pickpocket in the crowd, steering them into a souvenir shop a block from the theater. "Daddy will want to know what people are saying . . . and selling." The streets *were* overwhelming. Jo flipped through a pile of cheaply manufactured Jenny Lind ties on a table. Every shelf in every shop seemed lined with her friend's name or likeness.

Caroline lifted a can of Jenny Lind biscuits. "Think of it," she mused. "Someday her *voice* will be like this. They'll put it in a can, like biscuits, so anyone can buy it."

Jo blinked at the idea: there were limits to her disloyalty.

Caroline set down the biscuit tin, and Jo struggled to keep up.

"Think of it. Once only royalty could wear satin," Caroline said. "Now everyone can — anyone who can afford it."

Along with cigars, and opera vests, and sausages, Jo thought. *Five for a picayune.*

Not such a rare bird after all.

"I expect that will be a long time in the future," Jo said dutifully. "After Jenny's day."

Caroline looked up — shamed, at last, into silence. "Oh, don't mistake me. *Her* songs would cost a pretty penny, a fortune, while my can would come cheap. Boy, I get lost in my thoughts sometimes. Have I offended you? Do be frank and say if so. Please. Don't tell Daddy first. He would send me home and lock me up in Iranistan if he thought I'd stepped my bounds."

Jo smiled at the girl in the woman, a daughter before all. "Jenny wouldn't agree, but I admire your forward thinking. And besides," Jo said, "not everyone gets to be locked up in a palace."

It was Barnum's printed stationery — engraved with an image of his Moorish estate — that had decided Jenny on the tour. A man who owned such a place was not a mere adventurer, she had reasoned.

"Are you unhappy there?" Jo asked Caroline.

The question seemed to take Caroline by surprise.

"Not at home. It's just . . . that house. But I'll be married by next year." She drew a finger to her lips, and her voice dropped. "*Anything* to leave that house."

They were a few minutes late getting to the theater that night. Jo got Jenny situated in her dressing room while Caroline saw an usher about their box.

Wardrobe, at least, was easy. Jenny dressed simply, in white — no elaborate costumes, no makeup.

Her voice came from God, she liked to say; she sang for God, and it was her duty to use her gift to help others; her many charities would have agreed. But it was time for her to think of herself now, Jenny had confided after dinner, stunning Jo into silence.

Jo had half believed she couldn't do it, wouldn't do it. *You can have anyone. Anyone at all.*

The decision was made, and Jo couldn't stop thinking about what the consequences would be. Jenny wasn't the only one who had to think of herself now. Remembering their whispered conversation, how the serving staff had tiptoed about with ladles, pretending not to hear, upset her all over again. Jo excused herself to look at the crowd.

She walked to the stairs in her stiff new opera slippers—Jenny had picked them out in New York, knowing Jo preferred the kid-whites—and peeked inside the lit theater.

The boxes had open white balustrades, and ladies in both tiers of the dress circle and in the pit glistened with jewels. Most people in the audience were fanning themselves with Barnum's new programs, on sale in the lobby for twenty-five cents, with every song printed in Italian, German, Swedish, French, and English.

The St. Charles was a luxury theater, and Jenny would give thirteen performances under its dome, singing, as she always did, from her deepest self, often with her eyes closed. Normally Jo would walk her to the stage area, where Barnum took her arm after his introduction and escorted her onstage, but Jo refused to pander. Not today. Otto could do that work when he got here, and work he would.

The lights in the theater dimmed, and breathless silence gave way to applause. The orchestra, thirty-five musicians conducted by Benedict, filed out and performed their set, including Felix's "Wedding March" from *A Midsummer Night's Dream*. Jo knew that Jenny would be listening backstage in her dressing room with glassy eyes, numb. It was one thing to hear his masterpiece rehearsed day after day and another to hear it in full splendor.

It was agony sometimes, knowing as much as Jo did — so much that Otto didn't about his future bride. Worst of all was to know she couldn't spare him any of it. That time had passed.

When Jenny took the stage, the rafters rang with the thunder that attended her wherever she went. Jo was so tired of the same glorious program night after night after night, but to these multitudes, it was as fresh as a lily.

By the time Jenny cut early to her signature piece, "The Bird Song" by Taubert — performing with smiling archness to mimic the caroling of a bird, bouncing her voice here and there, and inciting waves of laughter — the crowed was ready to forgive her anything.

The Nightingale quit the stage in a shower of bouquets, refusing an encore, so the audience chanted for

Barnum — so loudly and so long that he couldn't refuse.
Jenny led him center stage amid cheers, and the showman bowed with all the genuine humility he kept hidden. Jo glanced up at Caroline, alone in their box now,
and her pride was visible even from a distance. Why
would she flee her fairy-tale home in Connecticut, Jo
wondered, when she so clearly adored her father?

What Jo wouldn't give to go home to her own
family.

A raucous brass band led by a bannered procession of
Fire Company No. 20, and another culled from the St.
Charles Orchestra, took separate routes to the Pontalba
buildings that night. Each accumulated a crowd, and
the combined ensemble pooled below Jenny's balcony,
serenading her by turns into the night. Jenny stepped
out from time to time, waving or clapping at the end
of a number, and after an hour or so, both bands and
their jolly entourages marched away, leaving a lonely,
welcome silence.

The show had been a grand success, Barnum ruled
as they said their good-nights in the hall outside Jenny's
suite and parted ways for the evening.

At breakfast, the showman read only the best
reviews aloud while the ladies fanned themselves. "'I
heard true music for the first time,'" he crooned, "'a
uniquely pure tone . . . you might say "celestial".'"

In his enthusiasm, though, he let one that offered

neither praise nor blame slip through: "'Her voice was not powerful,'" he read with a skeptic's shrug, "'but it was absolutely obedient. She tossed it about as jugglers do balls and seemed to have twenty voices at once.'"

Jenny commanded him to read that one again.

They all looked at her, Barnum unable to hide his bemusement.

Yes, Jenny demanded it in all things and people: obedience.

For once, their last night in New Orleans, Jenny slept like the dead, while Jo couldn't sleep at all.

Sometime after four a.m., she dragged a chair out to the balcony.

In the blessed silence, Jo gazed down at cobbles gleaming in the dim light from the gas lamps, at a stray dog nosing around an overturned ash bin, and at the wet confetti littering the street. She tried to shut out thoughts of the next stop on the tour, and the stops after that.

Now that her days on the tour were numbered, she wondered whose days they were. She had stood for so long beside Jenny, so firmly in her shadow, that she no longer remembered why she had refused him, why she had introduced the two of them in Germany after Felix died, why she had let Otto become Jenny's savior and not her own.

At sunrise, she stood barefoot on a cushion of

rotting flowers, warm in the heat, until the bells of St. Louis began to ring.

How many balconies? How many cities? How many pealing bells marking the day, or the passing of days, or the passing of human lives on that day? Josephine would sweep the wet petals away before Jenny woke, but for now she trod on them in her bare toes, kneading them as a cat does a blanket, and closed her eyes. She reached into the blind air to touch his untouchable face.

WE WILL ALWAYS
BE SISTERS

None of the ghosts that haunt houses are of the least
possible use. They plague people, but do no good.
They act like the spirits of departed monkeys.

—P. T. Barnum

When you had an elephant in your yard, it was difficult to be bored. But sometimes, to Helen's bewilderment, her sisters were, except the dead one.

Like Helen, Frances saw their home in the wilds of Connecticut for what it was, a palace of unique proportions, the playground of her days.

Helen was never as bewildered by seeing or sensing Frances as she should have been. The spritely presence, what remained of her sister, was familiar, soothing in a way Frances wasn't while alive.

Apart from the occasional chilling flash of mischief, Frances was like no haunting in a story. She was just *there*, not to be forgotten. She felt no sympathy for Helen or anyone and commanded secrecy.

As it stood, Helen had no one to gossip with, least of all about a ghost.

When they moved in four years ago, Daddy had named their home Iranistan. The public strayed all over its grounds. He insisted they should be allowed this liberty, though Mother found it intrusive (another reason to stay shut up in her dark drawing room). Pauline was only six and hated all that Helen loved — namely mud, feathers, and fur. The littlest's only ambitions were to look pretty, play with dolls, and court Daddy's favor, monopolizing him over his morning cocoa.

As for Caroline, Helen often found the question at the tip of her tongue when they were together — her big sister was her oldest confidante — but something held it back. Besides which, in two days' time, Caroline would marry Mr. David Thompson and leave Iranistan forever. Helen would be as good as alone then.

Her theory was that Frances attached to her because she could keep a secret. The ghost's one and strict demand was discretion. To stray from that compact was risky, and on the day of their elder sister's wedding, Helen would learn *how* risky. But for now, things were as usual.

She woke to the feeling of someone lying behind her, twirling a lock of her hair around a finger. Helen knew that if she reached back, there would be no finger. No hand, no tickle of breath — so she paid her quickened pulse no mind (it was better, in her experience, to pretend Frances wasn't there). She dressed hurriedly, eager to get outdoors, where the animals were.

Helen lived for the animals. They were the sun while Frances was the moon, moody and chill. On Mondays, the man Daddy called Mahout (though his real name was Mr. Bleeker) brought the elephant out to plow before the morning trains went by. Daddy wanted the factory girls and office grunts in every passenger car to see and remark on Barnum's elephant and resolve to bring their children to the American Museum on Saturday.

The elephant had no name. Daddy had devised a contest, but first he had to give the animal a heroic life story, something to set folks weeping and open their purses, and he never seemed to get around to it.

The elephant was a bull, but Helen had called him Jane since before she knew that. Jane was no fan of Frances. None of the animals were. On "Frances days," Helen kept a wide berth. She felt guilty making her usual rounds those mornings, as her companion sent silver pheasants scurrying under hydrangea and mandarin ducks streaking across the pond in a flurry of wings. With Frances trailing her round the fountain — one invisible hand dragging through the mucky water after Helen's — goldfish scattered.

With Frances by, Helen didn't dare enter the stables. Prince Albert the pig would cower, snuffling, in his hay. Bessie the cow, who liked to nibble the rich grass under Daddy's bedroom window, would startle as they passed, a wild glaze in her amber eyes.

Both Mother and Caroline complained — at twelve, they said, Helen was too old for such behavior — but it was her habit to roam out on fine mornings. Her Monday route included a jaunt through the meadow to contemplate Jane and wave at the trains.

That done, Helen strayed through seventeen acres of fruit trees, sandy evergreens, and shrubbery between the mansion and the sound, and wound her way back to the mansion, which never ceased to occupy her.

Daddy's sandstone country seat in Bridgeport had been modeled on the Royal Pavilion of King George IV, which he and Charlie had visited during their European tour. Iranistan was a fairy-tale palace with a Middle Eastern theme, all three stories of which Mother's clan found immodest and "ostentatious," a word that perfectly mirrored its meaning, Helen believed.

If she had friends to speak of, they would court her favor for the chance to loll on the big divan under the soaring onion dome or stroll piazzas in the shadow of Turkish towers and minarets. They would envy her this paradise. But Mother never took Helen and Pauline out in society, polite or otherwise, so friends and even enemies were scarce.

Sometimes she thought of Charlie—if anyone would understand about Frances, it would be Charlie—and wondered how he was, but he would not remember her now. He was General Tom Thumb, the biggest little star in Daddy's constellation, possibly the biggest little star in the entire world. He had no time for her (or Frances).

For the last year, Caroline had had a fiancé, who relieved the monotony somewhat, though the Bridgeport accountant was plenty monotonous if you asked Helen and of far less interest than the colored light pouring through stained-glass windows in Daddy's library—dancing on the library's Asian frescoes of spiny trees and cranes and elephants, that light was a thing of beauty—or the botanical mysteries in the octagonal greenhouse.

If only there were someone to share these riches with, one who did more than trail along mimicking her actions—sometimes Helen closed her eyes and pretended to be blind, her hands groping the familiar pillars and trellises—or shaking the leaves on a low-hanging branch to rain down petals or unripe apples.

On any given day, then, besides Frances (at her whim and discretion, of course; there was no predicting when she might turn up), Helen saw Pauline, her tutor, the housekeeper, the cook, the stablemen and groundskeepers, and sometimes Mother, unless Daddy was hosting someone famous like the Hutchinson Family Singers. Helen never knew which visitors were famous and which not unless Daddy announced it in advance or Mother let Pauline put on her best frock.

Helen liked it when people came, because Daddy would be home for a time and not "holed up," as Mother put it, in Manhattan. At home he was predictable. He walked mornings in the garden and napped after supper. Evenings, he read in his library. He might seem surprised to see you—if you turned up sniffing a rose or were found reading in a chair by the fire, bathed in colored light from the windows—but he welcomed you just the same.

More days than not, the faces blurring past on the morning train impressed Helen more than her family

did, though this was not true of tourists. The gates of
Iranistan were always open, and in pleasant weather,
carriages clattered past. Curiosity seekers came on foot
also, promenading under parasols through Helen's paradise and viewing her as decorative, like the grinning
stone satyrs around the carriageway.

With Caroline out of the picture, Helen might go
days with no one to remind her of the sound of her
own voice, unless Mother emerged from her drawing
room or Pauline laid down her dolls, much less someone to tell her secrets to.

Secrets weighed heavily on Helen.

In an unusual feat of physical exertion, Mother cor-
nered her the moment she came back from her rounds,
demanding to know why Helen had "done it."

Helen was confounded. That morning, before turning up in her favorite sister's bed, Frances had appar-
ently taken the trouble to open every bath spout on
the second story (a further wonder of Iranistan was
its modern heated bathrooms, including full showers
and tubs). The maid had found at least one tiled floor
flooded.

With wedding guests due to trickle in anytime,
Mother could barely keep her rage in check, though
she was trying; Helen could see that—theirs was a
fragile peace.

Clearly Helen was the culprit. No one else went
upstairs with Daddy not at home. The Barnum living

quarters were at ground level, and the girls were forbidden upstairs without adult supervision. There was a "Picture Room" on the second level full of valuable paintings, plus dozens of lavish guest chambers, not to mention her father's private study, lined in orange satin.

A floor above *that*, at the tip-top of the house, was a billiard room that doubled as a music chamber, and a grand ballroom, its shiny wooden floor inscribed with Daddy's motto, "Love God and be merry."

Pauline loved to waltz with her pretend princes up there during parties, but Helen liked the ballroom best in silence, when she could imagine the music and the dancers twirling and write and illustrate stories about them. And she often sneaked up the spiral staircase to the great central dome to take in the view of the whole grounds.

She could only stammer back while Mother accused her. "Wh-what?"

"What! *What*, she says. Why have you flooded the guest suites before the wedding party arrives?"

"I did no such thing!"

"Then who did?" challenged Mother. "Pauline?"

"Perhaps," said Helen sullenly. "You might ask her."

"Hardly," said Mother. Pauline stood just behind Mother, rocking her big dolly and holding it up, making it dance, making smacking noises with her lips.

"She's been with me the entire morning, playing with her dolls."

"Surprise."

"Excuse me?" demanded Mother, her eyes blazing.

Helen was not typically short with her mother, but she was still smarting from the events of the previous month. They had been reading in the sitting room one Sunday when one of Helen's many rescued cats trotted in with a dead mole and dropped it on the carpet at their feet.

Mother went berserk. "That's it. That cat must go. It's always *that* cat!" She turned away and began inexplicably weeping into the chair, her back shuddering as she told the fabric, "I will not have my Turkish carpets littered with filthy bodies—"

"But, Mother," Helen objected, "Clementine's pregnant!"

"Cats are always pregnant!" She whirled back. "It's a vicious killer."

"She's a *cat*." Helen leaped up and scooped the toothy mole with its little rigid limbs into her handkerchief. "She brings them to me as a gift," she explained. "She's being *nice* . . ."

"Nice? Put that foul thing down *at once*! You are as feral as the cat." Mother reached up and rang the servants' bell—over and over like a madwoman—rocking forward and back in her fury and frustration.

When the butler came, Mother ignored Helen,

instructing him over her desperate entreaties. Clementine lay in a luxurious arc with her bump showing, all innocence.

Helen sprang forward and scooped her up for her own protection, but the gray devil (as Helen called her favorite) didn't like being held close. She wriggled and scratched Helen before leaping down and into the butler's trap, a picnic basket with flaps. He clapped the lid closed, holding it flat while Clem yowled and scratched the weave.

"You'll need wire," Mother said in the cold voice Helen knew meant business. "You can still catch Mr. Barnum on his way out for the morning, George. Tell him I said he must take Helen's cat to live at the museum."

Helen kicked the wall.

"He won't regret it," Mother told George. "She's a good mouser."

"Daddy will leave her somewhere!" Helen objected. "He won't bring her all the way in on the train—"

"He will if you ask him to." Mother nodded to the butler, turning back sternly. "You are too softhearted, Helen."

And that was the end of it.

It was also the last time for nearly two weeks that Helen spoke to her mother.

Her patience now, under scrutiny, was strained at best. "I didn't *do* anything." She spoke with as much softness and sincerity as she could muster. She *was* the obvious choice.

"Then you would have me accuse the staff?"

Helen winced. *No.* But what could she do? Blame Frances? The imp had conveniently vanished back on the lawn. Or that was where Helen's memory of her — her dim knowing, a step below awareness — stopped.

If Caroline were here, she would know what to do, how to distract Mother from these accusations. She was the politician among the sisters, a knack cultivated by observing Daddy at close range. She was the only one in the family who traveled with him, helped on tour, the only one to fight for his affections.

Though it sometimes saddened her to give up on others, Helen was content with her own company (*But so much of it?* a voice in her head interjected; it was one thing to *choose* her own company, but after the wedding?). She was clever with words but not people, and unlike Caroline, she lacked the will to be accounted for. Spoiled Pauline never had to try.

Mother's face was an alarming shade of red. "You will sit there — right *there* in that chair — and wait for your father to come home. *You* can explain why you flooded the floors just in time for the arrival of your sister's wedding party."

Helen made her hands into a steeple in her lap to keep from gnawing the edge of her thumb. The habit scandalized Caroline, and it was nearly Caroline's wedding day. The least Helen could do for her was not "savage her own flesh."

"Where is Caroline, by the way?" Mother demanded. "David should know better than to keep her out all week when there are preparations to be made. . . . Why must *I* do everything?"

It was a rhetorical question. Mother's questions usually were. Sometimes it seemed to Helen that no one spoke directly to one another anymore, only to themselves. At least with Frances, she didn't have to pretend.

Caroline wasn't here to defend her. As of the weekend, Caroline would no longer be available to defend her at all.

In fact, it dawned on Helen that her last substantive conversation with her sister had been over a year ago, when Caroline returned from the Jenny Lind tour. They were laughing together over some Prince of Humbug reference in a *Herald* editorial while Caroline scribbled in her journal. Out of the blue, Caroline sighed and set her coffee cup down much too hard in its saucer.

"One thing about Daddy," Helen offered conversationally, feeling her sister's boredom like a blade. "He's never dull."

"No, but we are," Caroline said, "which is why he's entombed us in this pretty place."

"Does he keep us here because we're dull, or are we dull because he keeps us here?"

"Now you're a philosopher."

"At your service," said Helen with a mock bow, walking her breakfast plate to a tray stand to be helpful.

"What else is there to do?" Caroline lamented. The excitement of the Jenny Lind tour had taken its toll. "I miss New York. I miss the museum."

Helen felt she should support her sister, who was older and cosmopolitan, after all, but the truth was she liked it here. She nodded, but Helen would never choose anywhere else. To even suggest it felt disloyal, as if the house were listening.

Helen sat on her hands, awaiting her father's wrath. She watched the hustle and bustle mount. The housekeeper bullied a temporary staff about. Rugs and blankets had their slappings and airings, flowers were cut and arranged, silver candlesticks and place settings and brocade tablecloths emerged from locked trunks. It was a dusty business, but little by little, as the light waned, the dust cleared. Helen felt her anxiety mounting by the moment, too, and wondered . . . just a little . . . what it might feel like to tell the truth. To lay blame where blame belonged for once and point a finger at the blank air. *It was her.* Frances. *She's right* there.

But Frances wasn't right there. She had made her mischief and moved on. She was a fly-by-night, a flutter-by, a free thing. Helen envied this incarnation of Frances, who would never have to sit for hours in a chair, awaiting judgment. Frances would be blameless all her cursed days on earth.

When Caroline got home, Helen was so urgent she nearly wept. She did weep some, theatrically, into her sister's perfumed collar. For this dear safe friend would abandon her soon with Pauline, who could do no wrong and was about as useful as one of her dolls, and Mother, who hardly counted, and with Frances, whom no one else could see or sense. And if they didn't believe in Frances, they could hardly believe in *her*, since Helen belonged as much to Frances as anyone.

Flush with her busy social calendar and budding nuptials, Caroline was all munificence. "Come." She held out her hand and walked Helen up to Mother's door. They both paused to take a deep breath as in the old days, then walked into the room, where Pauline was sprawled on the floor with her dollhouse.

Helen sat on a hard chair while Caroline breezed into the attached water closet. Mother was in there unpapering her ringlets before their dinner with the pastor. They conversed in quiet tones while Helen felt her name on their lips, her fate in their hands, or someone's.

Pauline was humming to herself, stuffing her favorite dolly into a flounced dress.

Helen shifted on the chair, studying the miniature house on the floor beside her sister. As detailed in its way as Iranistan, down to the papered walls and tiny furniture, it was modeled on a dollhouse Daddy had seen and admired in the home of the queen of England.

Helen was sometimes dimly aware of Someone hovering over everything—Pastor Tom would say God, but Helen wasn't so sure—a mischievous presence spoiled by infinite power, directing them. *Toying* was the word, moving them around. Some days, she imagined this Someone staring down, a finger on its cosmic chin. *What to do today? What to do.*

She felt that mind starting little fires here and there for the doll-folk to put out, keeping itself entertained, a bit like Clementine with a grasshopper on the lawn or Frances with her pranks.

Then she noticed something different about Pauline's dollhouse: it had an extension. "Where did you get that?" she demanded, standing for a fraction of a second but catching herself. Mother would be furious to find her out of her chair.

Pauline began humming under her breath. Helen knew this game. Every time Helen spoke, Pauline's humming would get louder.

"That doesn't belong to you. Hand it here."

"No," Pauline said primly. "It's mine."

"It's not. It belonged to Frances."

Pauline pinched her face up. "It's *mine.*"

"No. It isn't. Charlie sent it for Frances . . . for her birthday."

"Who is Charlie?" Pauline demanded in a quavery voice. "Who is *Frances*?"

Helen leaped up.

WHO IS FRANCES?

Helen clapped a hand hard over her sister's mouth. She was already in trouble.

"No one. Mother will tell you someday, but only if you keep very quiet and wait until winter to ask. Are you ready to be quiet?"

Helen was used to feral cats; she knew just how to hold her hand over a bratty child's mouth so as not to be bitten. "I can wait all day like this," she said nonchalantly. "I can hold my hand here all day."

The eyes blazed rebellion, but eventually Pauline relented, nodding, and Helen released her hand and hopped back onto the chair.

Pauline had white marks all over her pink face. She stuck out her tongue and went back to work, fussing with her baby's frock.

Helen would rescue the puppet theater from Pauline's clutches later, when the room was empty. She would hide it high on the shelves in Daddy's library.

Caroline startled her out of her thoughts, extending a hand again. She walked Helen out and into the twilit garden arm in arm.

Caroline's generosity on this day, two days before she would desert Helen forever, was welcome but suspect.

"Mother won't tell him. I said have mercy . . . that you are jealous and sad to see me go. That this is a difficult time for you."

"Jealous?" Helen snapped back. "Never." She would not speak the words on her lips, but they were an unkind assessment of a certain Bridgeport accountant.

"Sad, then. We will always be sisters," Caroline said, pausing and lifting her hand in formal fashion. "We will always have each other."

"Caroline," Helen began, guarding the urge to ask outright. "Have you ever felt uneasy . . . at Iranistan? Afraid?"

"If by afraid you mean that I might die of boredom? Yes."

"No, I mean—"

"What?" Caroline snapped, impatient now. Her generosity was on the clock, on a schedule. This was "appease my dear sister" time, not "let's exchange secrets" time. "*What* do you mean, Helen? Hurry! Pastor Tom will be here soon, and I need to dress."

Helen brought her voice low and stepped close. "Do you ever feel we aren't alone?"

There it was, clear as day on Caroline's face: a glimmer of knowing. "I have no idea what you mean." She set her mouth and turned away.

Caroline went and just kept going, leaving Helen in a tide of doom and dread. She felt a heat in her face, for she was being watched, just as she was watching the retreating back of her sister, the bride, and with the same intensity.

When Daddy had first moved them into the mansion, Helen was only eight, but she had a vivid memory of the housewarming party. Some thousand guests had attended — from New York elite to Bridgeport rabble — and if Caroline had any say, and she usually did, her wedding would be just as big. Daddy would make a show of it.

The bride had tried to engage her in the planning process, but Helen had maintained a decided lack of curiosity until today — though she had been thinking, a lot, about sisterhood.

One of Helen's earliest memories of Frances wasn't even of Frances.

It was an infamous day in family history when Helen and Caroline sneaked out of the apartment to see Daddy's Fejee Mermaid on their own. The monkey-like beast behind the glass, in all its frozen agony, had reminded Helen of Frances home in her cradle, wailing when she was hungry, when she couldn't get enough milk . . . enough love . . . enough air in greedy little lungs.

The only other things she recalled about that day were her terror of the crowds and of being lost, and holding Caroline's sweaty hand, and the troubling thought that surfaced while she gaped up at that glass case, one Helen would carry with her for the rest of her life: *We are all his creatures.*

But Frances was free now.

Frances belonged to no one.

The house was filling up with guests. Carriages kept arriving, and many had traveled vast distances. Trunks full of formal wear and no doubt costly gifts were heaped in the carriageway when Helen woke up, and the staff had been roasting meats and plucking fowl and baking tarts for days. The rich smells rose up and up from the kitchen.

The ceremony and celebration would be that evening. The fire broke out while their father was in downtown Bridgeport for a shave. The roof blazed a mean orange as smoke wheeled from the dome, and the maids' shouting sent everyone out to the lawn in various states of undress, carrying what they could.

When David Thompson stormed into the barbershop shouting, "Mr. Barnum, Iranistan is in flames! The roof is on fire!" Daddy jumped up from the chair and both men bolted for the wagon. Jacketless, with one half of his face still lathered and the other shaved, Daddy lashed the horses and called out to his future son-in-law over the clatter and wind: "Never mind!"

He could hardly look at the young man, he said later, David was so pale and stricken, but he seemed to settle back and accept his circumstances as they thundered along. "We can't help these things! The house may be burned, but if no one's harmed, you'll be married tonight, even if we perform the ceremony in the coach house!"

They shouted on their way past the fire station for the company to hurry their machine out to Iranistan.

Black smoke was rolling from the roof when they entered the gates. Luckily, men had been repairing the roof earlier in the day, and their ladders were propped and ready against the house. A number of groundsmen were already stationed on ladders and the roof, handing on buckets of water. When the brigade arrived, these combined efforts paid off, and the fire was tamed without serious damage.

After the fire was safely extinguished and the trunks that had been hauled out onto the lawn returned to the rooms that were dry enough, the party began early and in earnest. Caroline kept her humor about it, for the ceremony felt incidental to the day's adventures. "I kept my calm," Daddy told them all during a toast to the happy couple, "for David's sake, but you can't imagine my distress. All I could think was that someone might get killed or injured trying to save things from the fire. And of course," he said, bowing to Caroline, "I thought of the sore disappointment a

calamity would cause the young couple and our welcome guests."

Iranistan had come as near to destruction as it could
and still escape. "But escape it did." Daddy winked at
Caroline, who blushed. "Cheers!"

"Cheers!"

Helen stood in back, behind the sighing crowd,
the ladies dabbing handkerchiefs to their eyes as Mr.
Barnum pulled his daughter into a bear hug.

Helen closed her eyes but saw their faces anyway —
not smiling or weeping with joy but pale with disbelief,
as they had looked earlier, out on the lawn, in the faint
glow of flame — and her shame sickened her.

That night, when the guests were tucked in, when
the house was a cocoon of shifting and snoring, Helen
stole to the top of the spiral staircase.

She sat on its upper step without a sound, mouse-
still, with an acrid smell in her nostrils, and looked at
the moon through the black hole in the ceiling. "I'm
sorry," she whispered, but the only sound was branches
bending in the wind, the flapping of a charred shingle.

THE FAIRY WEDDING

I do not propose to assist in entertaining Tom Thumb. My notions of duty, perhaps, are somewhat different from yours.
— Robert Todd Lincoln

If his friends at Harvard could see him now, lurking outside the East Room as if he didn't belong there, as if he hadn't been invited.

"Shall I announce you, sir?"

Robert stepped back from the flow of arrivals and shook his head. How to coast through the hall without being seen by the people he normally jockeyed to be seen by? He could wait for the room to fill, he supposed—and it would—and then stroll past incognito. If he looked purposeful enough, anyone who knew him would think he was heading to his father.

He wished he could ape his brothers and just duck behind the velvet drapes. Robert had been born at the Globe Tavern, his parents' first married home, a four-dollar-a-month furnished room. Tad and Willie were the indulged ones, the first children ever to live in the big white house on the hill. They did as they pleased, racing up and down the great halls, spilling cider on Mother's carpets, dodging statesmen and generals, and shrieking to high heaven. In their heyday, they built a play fort on the roof of the mansion, firing on Confederate soldiers across the Potomac, and played hide-and-seek among the diplomats at receptions. Even their pets had free run: the pony they rode around the grounds; their yellow dog, Fido; the goat that slept on Tad's bed.

From the moment Father took office and the Lincolns claimed the Executive Mansion, the boys had the run of the place. But this was before the Unspeakable, before Father fetched Robert "home" from Harvard — almost a year ago to the day — to stand by his brother in the metal box with a silver plate inscribed "William Wallace Lincoln. Born December 21st, 1850. Died February 20th, 1862."

Unlike Willie's funeral, which had closed down Washington, tonight's reception was hastily staged. Invitations had gone out only that morning.

All during breakfast, Mother had pleaded with him to attend, while he skimmed accounts of the New York wedding (if the spectacle could be called a wedding) in yesterday's papers. Barnum's "fairy" romance — the "Loving Lilliputians," the "Little Queen of Beauty" and her "Fairy Prince" — had knocked the war off the front pages two days running.

Robert couldn't in good conscience attend the reception for Tom Thumb, he told his mother. *Not in a million years.*

She gave him that *Come off your high horse, sir, and join the rest of us* look but immediately smoothed her hoop-skirts, cleared her throat, and assumed a motherly bearing again. Robert had learned to expect the viper under that basket of skirts. The president's assistant private secretary hadn't nicknamed Mrs. Mary Todd Lincoln "Hellcat" for nothing.

"You recall when we took the boys to Barnum's Museum," she badgered, "don't you? During the campaign? Remember we saw the General's tiny uniform on display there?"

He sipped his coffee.

"Robert? In New York?" she prompted him.

"I remember, yes."

"Well, I want to see the real thing. I want to see the tiny man. Taddy wants to see the real thing, too. Need I remind you . . . we've had so little joy. You at least do not live and labor in this glass house."

That almost bought his sympathy, but she never could quit while she was ahead. "You must know," she pressed on, "the wedding is the talk of New York — and now Washington. Everyone says General Tom Thumb has been feted by royalty in the Old World — why shouldn't the wife of the president of his native land smile upon him, too? Why not, Bob?"

Robert heard her anxiety mounting, an unstoppable force.

"You at least are not expected to be always cheerful," she snapped, "always available. This is no kind of home."

And so you invite a troupe of players in, he thought (he would never speak the words aloud, but *honestly*), *on*

more or less the anniversary of Willie's death? And a frenzy of
curiosity mongers?

"Do this much for your mother," said a voice close
to his ear.

Father had coasted in late, as he often did for meals,
appearing out of nowhere and folding his tall frame
into a chair. He spread his napkin in his lap as Robert
turned with a helpless shrug. "I'm sorry."

There was no more to be said. A strained silence
ensued.

Robert resisted the urge to sulk. He had left home
before the presidency, at sixteen, to study at Phillips
Exeter Academy, advancing quickly to Harvard. He was
no stranger to the mansion but sometimes felt like one.
He slept in the state guest room, the Prince of Wales
Room. He slept poorly and too late most mornings,
waking to find that the life of the house had gone on
without him.

At the holidays or when events called him home,
his mother's friend and dressmaker, Elizabeth, greeted
him warmly. She often seemed happier to see him than
his own parents did and kept Robert well informed. It
surprised him how much it hurt to hear that when the
president wasn't brooding over the war, or disabled
by melancholy, he found time for the others; he spent
quiet evenings in the parlor, she said, sprawled on the
floor reading newspapers or wrestling with Tad, Willie,
and Fido on the expensive rugs Mother had put in to

beautify the mansion. He brought the boys with him to visit Union troops camped along the Potomac.

If Robert regretted that his father had never wrestled with him as a child (he couldn't remember him ever touching his face or his arm; Robert sometimes thought even a whipping would have done), he wouldn't say. As firstborn, Robert had always been a little man, buttoned up; he was a priggish, cross-eyed child who kept his own counsel, and his family let him. Should it surprise him now that his father saved his warm affections for the others?

No, but pride and natural reserve made Robert determined to set the record straight. When the press asked, he told the truth: "When I was young he was almost constantly away from home, attending courts or making political speeches. . . . I was lucky to have ten minutes of quiet talk with him."

And it was not exactly true, what Mother said — that he had no responsibilities. Robert was a public figure in spite of himself, even in faraway Cambridge. He was a celebrity by association, not vocation or choice. The press badgered him, too, and Robert hated the attention as much as he hated to be forgotten. If he kept to himself, he was seen as haughty, a snob; if he tried to profit from his father's position, the world called him pampered, a favorite, and wasn't that a laugh?

*   *   *

He watched the elite of Washington line up outside the East Room — each paused in their tracks, waiting to be announced to a bogus reception — and remembered the last time he had stood here. A few moments later he had found himself before a coffin, dabbing his brother's cold cheek with his knuckle. He had been glad all the mirrors in the East Room were covered for the funeral, glad he would not glance up and catch his own gaunt face in the glass. They were all specters in that room: family and friends but also cabinet secretaries, foreign dignitaries, members of Congress, and generals — all casting sly glances at their weakened leader. Even Confederate president Jefferson Davis had sent condolences.

Willie was "too good for this earth," his father would moan, right in front of people. "It is hard, hard to have him die."

Willie had a way, the pastor reminded all assembled in the East Room that day, of "entwining" himself around their hearts. To Robert, the comment seemed macabre, with Mother unwilling to budge from her bed upstairs. She wouldn't come down to see her son buried, though she had clutched and clawed at the little bouquet of flowers that was fitted into Willie's dead hands by the embalmer, bruised petals peppering her nightdress. It would be months before she emerged again. Yes, Willie had entwined himself around her heart: a vine of piercing thorns.

The press had crowned Will "the Little Favorite" a long time ago, and his presence lurked everywhere, though Mother had tried to banish it. She had sent whatever reminded her of Willie away, including his friends — Taddy's, too, as if poor Tad weren't neglected enough these days — and Father was too busy with his own loss, and choreographing a war, to intervene.

Tad had survived the same fever that had taken Willie. He took up the mantle of "favorite" after that.

One short year later, Robert was forced to make it clear that this reception — circus, more like — was beneath his dignity, beneath the dignity of his father's office. But that was at breakfast, and as the hour approached, curiosity was getting the better of him. Wasn't that what these show people did? Prey on curiosity?

He couldn't help but wonder how his father would fare with the tiny man and his equally tiny wife. Robert had no trouble imagining his mother. She would fawn and laugh too loudly, but the President?

Robert had waffled, but as word circulated that the newlyweds were arriving in their silver coach (a wedding gift from Tiffany and Co., mobbed by pedestrians, of course), he was intrigued and took his chance. "No announcement, please, Jim." He ducked in past the butler and stationed himself against a wall. The craning crowd would conceal him better than a curtain.

Robert located his father beneath the big chandelier

and watched from afar, watched the president watching the room.

Senator Wilson, Representative Crittenden, secretaries Chase and Stanton, and generals Butler and Clay were among the few dozen politicians and ranking Union officers, most with their families, on hand for the show.

To see these gentlemen of distinction buzzing with boyish excitement *was* worth the price of admission, Robert thought. He heard a distinctive voice in the crowd and saw Gideon Welles, secretary of the navy, lean to his companion. "He's from my home state, you know."

His companion was Grace Greenwood, one of the first women to gain a press pass to Congress and the mansion, here scribbling away no doubt under her pen name, Sara Jane Lippincott, and hanging on the secretary's every word.

Charles Stratton and his tiny bride, Lavinia Warren Stratton, had made Washington a stop on their three-year honeymoon tour. Any moment, they would enter the East Room attended by the crushing fanfare that went wherever they did.

All of New York society had clamored to be invited to the wedding, and while Mr. Barnum had had the decency not to charge admission to the ceremony itself, tickets to the reception went for a whopping seventy-five dollars each to the first five thousand to apply.

A public outrage, some said. How dare the Yankee showman profane the house of God and use the Church and its holy rites to advertise his business? But even after Trinity Church shut him out, Barnum staged the wedding he wanted at Grace Episcopal. Two thousand guests were invited, from governors to tycoons. Police lined Broadway and the procession route, which the city closed to traffic to better manage the thousands of onlookers.

Gazing around now, Robert could only imagine the pandemonium. The energy in the East Room was palpable and, to him, mysterious. What power was it that made otherwise sane and sober people of good breeding behave like fools? Never mind that men were dying by scores on battlefields — whole fields full, splayed, their faces frozen in agony. Less than two years ago, Union troops had been quartered in this very room, with their soiled socks lining every banister.

Robert followed newspaper accounts of the war with tremulous fury. He wanted to serve the Union. Badly. He wanted it so much it made him sick some days. It was a ringing in his ears, an itch in his blood. But Mother wouldn't hear of it. His failure rankled even Father's political allies, and when Senator Harris last polled Mother, she shot back, "Robert is not a shirker — the fault is mine. He will stay in college a little longer.... An educated man can serve his country with more intelligent purpose than an ignoramus."

Robert tried his case every time he came to visit, but Mother held firm: "We have lost one son," she would say, and the subject was closed. Unless Father was in the room to urge, "But many a poor mother has given up all her sons, and ours is not more dear to us than the sons of others are to their mothers."

"That may be," she shot back, "but I cannot have Robert exposed to danger. His plea is noble, but I could not bear it . . . if he didn't come back to us."

Robert supposed he should be happy to see his mother busy and engaged, but it was hard to begrudge her even this much. He would never say so aloud, but she could be silly — in and out of her grief — and the miniature bride and groom weren't the worst of it: word was that Mother was letting spiritualists into the house to hold séances, charlatans pumping her parents' heads full of dark presentiment and stirring unrest. As if Father didn't have enough to worry about, holding the Union together. Encouraging his dreams and prophecies did no good. It was President Lincoln's rational mind, his native brilliance, that the nation required now, not the hick superstitions his cabinet mocked when he was out of earshot.

Robert was good at staying within earshot. It didn't pay, in this cutthroat world, to court ignorance, though there were so many ridiculous conversations in play, he couldn't be bothered keeping them all straight.

Was this what it felt like to be a spy? Here he stood,

in the shadows, making a study of the president and First Lady while they awaited visiting dignitaries. Ha.

When at last the hush fell, it was a relief.

The butler stepped in at eight o'clock sharp and announced, "Mr. and Mrs. Charles Stratton!"

The newlyweds strolled into the East Room from the corridor, advancing through the parting sea of guests with what one reporter would call "a pigeon-like stateliness," stopping where Father stood waiting, with Mother and Tad behind him, to welcome them.

Robert supposed it had been the same when the diminutive wedding party — including Mrs. Stratton's also-tiny sister, Minnie Warren, as bridesmaid and Commodore Nutt, the "new" Tom Thumb, as best man — arrived outside Grace Church. The papers said the police had to manage a stampede and that when the group entered the church, an "uprising ensued." Dignity went out the window. Guests stood on the seats to see over the heads of their neighbors; some brought stools, propped them on the benches, and stood on those. "As the little party toddled up the aisle," Robert had read, "irrepressible audible giggles ran through the church." *This is my solemn vow . . .*

After the ceremony, the hordes on foot chased the carriage to the Metropolitan Hotel, where Mr. and Mrs. Stratton stood on a grand piano to receive their guests. In the crowd were Vanderbilts, Astors, and their ilk, a dazzle of gems and furs.

The famous Shakespearean actor Edwin Booth had presented these "thimblesful of humanity" (Robert's favorite absurd endearment in the press) slippers embroidered by his own hand as a wedding gift.

As the couple paused now, with great pomp and circumstance, they looked up — up, up — into the craggy face of their nation's leader.

Smiling, Father took the bride's hands — gingerly, as if he might crush the dainty fingers cradled in his bony white-gloved ones — and then shook the groom's. "You have left me completely in the shade," he told Tom Thumb.

The General and his bride were on every mind in Washington.

Father bowed to the bride. "Mrs. Stratton," he said, loudly enough for the breathless room to hear, "I wish you much happiness in your union."

He presented the newlyweds to Mother, his tone courteous and natural and free of mockery. How he managed it, Robert would never know. To his not-yet-twenty-year-old mind, the fuss of weddings was uniform; this reception was no different, just exaggerated. *Absurd* was the word that came to mind, but *distasteful* worked, too.

Words came easily to Robert, though here again Willie won the day. He had published a poem in the *National Republican* about a family friend lost in battle and, from then on, got credit for inheriting Father's way with a phrase. How *would* Willie feel today? Robert agonized, watching Mother corral Tad with one arm. Had she no decorum? No shame?

Mother's free hand flitted like a moth around Lavinia Warren Stratton in her orange blossoms, diamonds, and pearls, but never lighted.

Mother wanted badly to touch her dress, he could see — lay hands on the fairy luminosity — but it was obvious the plump and regal Mrs. Stratton brooked no fools.

Tom Thumb shone, too, with glittering breast pins, shiny patent-leather shoes, and white kid gloves. Robert had learned a thing or two at boarding school and knew sartorial splendor when he saw it, but all he could focus on was his mother's flouncy pink dress with its plunging neckline.

When she wasn't in mourning costume, Mother tended toward manic self-display. She spent a fortune on gowns, hats, and jewelry, and Robert once overheard a guest at a state dinner ask whether that was "a flowerpot balanced on her head." His companion marveled that a woman "who had once milked her own cows" should now insist on "displaying her own milking apparatus" to all and sundry.

Mother's wardrobe and spending habits, the questionable salon she kept (abuzz with scandal and scoundrels) in the Blue Room, and the fact that she thumbed her nose at the press, made reporters and political enemies quick to brand her a harpy, a Confederate spy (those Southern Todds), or worse. That so notable and cultured a woman should be so erratic, with the nation in crisis, was unforgivable.

Apart from his ghastly pale gloves, Father wore black. His expression was respectful and bemused. If you didn't watch closely, didn't know his face the way Robert did, you might miss the glint of sorrow in his eyes. It came and went as the introductions droned on.

Others were inching nearer the famous group under the chandelier, the better to eavesdrop before the Marine Band went full blast. Robert followed suit. It was easy to stay hidden in the crowd, though he kept a furrowed brow to discourage passing conversation.

After an attendant removed the bride's train, Father led the couple to the sofa, lifting the General up and placing him at his left side while Mother did the same for Mrs. Stratton, placing her at her right, so the little couple sat squarely between them with legs extended. Father watched with a twinkle in his eye as statesmen and warriors came forward to shake the newlyweds' hands.

When someone asked the groom how he found married life, with so many curious fans in tow, his voice dropped suggestively. "Nothing short of a double lock and a pair of patent bolts has proved sufficiently powerful to preserve the sanctity of our bedchamber."

"And Washington?"

"Most congenial," said Tom Thumb, smiling at his wife. "Tomorrow we'll tour an army encampment on Arlington Heights across the Potomac with Lavinia's brother Benjamin, of the Fortieth Massachusetts Regiment." There was a scattering of applause. Was her brother also a dwarf? Robert wondered. He had never imagined sideshow performers with brothers or wives or fathers. A dwarf could serve the Union, it seemed, but not the president's own son.

Hanging on Mother's sleeve, Tad made a study of the bride. "Mother," he said, "if you were a little woman like Mrs. Stratton, you would look just like her."

Robert smiled at that, as did many who had inched close enough to hear. Tad's guilelessness had its uses, and for a moment, Robert felt almost guilty standing outside the family circle, lurking back here in the crowd like an onlooker. He smiled again as Tad in his loud voice compared the newlyweds to their father. "Isn't it funny that Father is so tall and Mr. and Mrs. Stratton are so little?"

"My boy," Father replied, "Dame Nature sometimes delights in doing funny things. You need not seek for any other reason"— he gestured from himself to the General —"for here you have the long and short of it."

The space under the chandelier erupted in laughter, and as the distinguished men formed a welcoming circle around the tiny dignitaries, Robert felt more and more sidelined. It was a simple fix, of course — just a few short steps. He could take his place beside his family, kiss Mother's cheek, and all would be forgiven.

But there he stood, two layers back in the crowd.

Making small talk, Father asked the General how he ought to conduct the war against the Rebels. Tom Thumb leaned in, puffing on a very fine-smelling cigar. "My friend Barnum," he said, "would settle the whole affair in a month."

What an American idea, Robert mused: a Prince of Humbug running the war. The showman had come through bankruptcy in one piece, and a great many other obstacles, too, including the loss of his Moorish mansion in Bridgeport, which had burned to the ground back in 1857.

"Have you never been called to active duty, General?" a man asked, and Robert winced. He couldn't place the man's face, but the question cut like a blade, though the star took it in stride, and Father teased: "His duty now is in the matrimonial field; he will serve with the home guard."

Robert turned his face to the wall, afraid the man who had asked the question might spot him and take the opportunity to belabor the point.

"I wish all of my generals were as good," Father added (not entirely in jest, Robert knew).

Refreshments arrived, and Tad offered a chair as a table so the distinguished little guests could reach their cake, wine, and ices. They accepted graciously, and after a nibble and a bit more banter, took a quiet promenade by themselves up and down the drawing room, clasping outstretched hands as they went.

Father watched that shrewd little pair with a puzzled—and puzzling, to Robert—smile on his face. Then he beamed at Mother. Robert felt in that instant the weight of it all as his father must feel it, the burden of human sympathy, for he treated everyone with forthright dignity, even those who tested him the most—people like his dear wife, who wore the words "Love Eternal" inside the ring he gave her. He never seemed to judge or talk down to another human soul, though many despised him for it.

The president had agreed to this show for "Mother's" sake without a second thought and then found the goodness in it, as Willie would have done.

The son ached for the father then, for himself, for the distance between them and the fact that, unlike Willie, Robert would never be so simple, so good. Watching his mother bend down to speak to Tom Thumb, laughing like a girl, Robert felt the sting of shame.

For months, the mere mention of Willie's name had been enough to send their mother into violent fits of weeping. During one of the worst of these, Father walked her to a window overlooking the asylum and gestured. "Mother, do you see that large white building on the hill yonder?" he asked. "Try and control your grief, or it will drive you mad, and we may have to send you there."

Father had had to hire a nurse to tend to her, and with the president's permission, Robert summoned his aunt Elizabeth, who had a brisk way with her sister (Robert was close to the Todds, and though Elizabeth's visit had ended badly, with Mother feeling ridiculed, he was proud of the role he had played in keeping their family balanced).

That morning over breakfast, when Mother had told him her haphazard plan for tonight's reception . . . he hated the thought that came next, so cruel under the circumstances, with Mother unwell, but no less the truth: *The inmates* are *running the asylum.*

She would never again enter the bedroom where Willie died or the downstairs Green Room, where they had embalmed his body. Until just lately, Mother had kept the mansion and herself muffled in black crepe, with no heart to see to her duties or curb public intrusions (things were so bad that vandals had taken to cutting out the delicate medallions from her lace curtains for souvenirs).

When Robert had looked down at Willie's still,

small form in that coffin a year ago, he blamed his brother for the attributes others prized in him, the ones Pastor Gurley spoke of in his eulogy.

Willie was, the pastor said, a "child of bright intelligence and peculiar promise." Just after the inauguration, when Robert couldn't get back to Harvard fast enough, the *New York Herald* had written an exposé of the president's eldest son: "He does everything very well, but avoids doing anything extraordinary. He doesn't talk much; he doesn't dance different from the other people; he isn't odd in any way."

The very opposite of peculiar promise.

Willie was the heir, the most like Father, the promise broken.

At half past nine, the newlyweds left the mansion and repaired to Willard's, where they would receive the press and friends.

As the East Room began to empty out, Robert moved with the last of the crowd. Then he turned on his heel and walked back in again, as if only just arriving. He would apologize. He would take his place at the heart of his family, in the heart of his nation, in the throes of a great and terrible war.

But his tired parents, socially rusty after a year of mourning, had taken another exit. The room was bare and silent but for the movements of two gloved waiters, darting here and there with trays, collecting glassware and soiled napkins.

"Good night, sir," one said, pausing to bow.

Robert saluted and left them to their work.

AN EXTRAORDINARY SPECIMEN OF MAGNIFIED HUMANITY

Do not endeavor to shine in all companies. Leave room for your hearers to imagine something within you beyond all you have said.

— Arthur Martine, Martine's Hand-Book of Etiquette, and Guide to True Politeness

When you are bigger, your joys are bigger, too, and your sorrows. You must work doubly hard to contain them.

This is what Mum always said. So from the time Anna was a child, she strove to be a model of deportment: demure, delicate, poised. Etiquette made order in a disorderly universe. It was her structure and her refuge.

On this day, Anna would lose her poise. She would lose everything, nearly — though she didn't know it yet as she stepped from her oversize carriage and helped Lavinia down, waving the driver away.

Whenever the friends lunched together, they did so in a closed room at a tavern, a respectable establishment, of course, though never a fashionable one. This was a pity, since they might have enjoyed seeing and being seen like other prominent New Yorkers, but in their case it was impossible *not* to be seen — and mobbed. Lavinia was in no way inclined to entertain the public for free. They could very well pay for the privilege, she always said, and Vinnie's stage appearances were rare these days. Lavinia and her husband, Charles, known to the masses as General Tom Thumb, were rich and famous enough to retire.

Anna still worked hard for her living.

During any given day she might be seen—should be seen, Mr. B. urged—traversing the city in her specially built carriage. Her transport was so large it took a pair of irritable Clydesdales to pull it, and it attracted the idle as the Pied Piper did rats, leading them back to the corner of Broadway and Ann Street and the famed American Museum.

Today Anna sent the carriage away so they wouldn't be found out and followed into the restaurant.

When she first arrived at the museum, the little folk had intrigued her. Anna had known none in Nova Scotia, and they were as exotic to her as she was to people of average height.

From the start, Mr. B. liked to pair Anna onstage with Commodore Nutt (Anna's "wee counterpart," Mum called him, who had his own carriage shaped like a walnut and harnessed to Shetland ponies).

Mr. B. loved contrast—tall and small, thin and portly, dark and albino—and was forever dreaming up new ways to coin a surprise. "Leave it to the professionals," Charles once advised. "If you're favored and fortunate—and you are, dear—that's clear—Barnum will display you to your best advantage and see you're well paid for it."

The General should know, Anna thought.

"That's why we stay," he had said firmly. "It's why we come back."

*   *   *

Lavinia kept an active social calendar, but when she was in the city, to Anna's delight, she often made the young Canadian giantess her first call.

Vinnie knew Anna's performance schedule and would surprise her while she was rehearsing backstage or up in her suite reading. "I've already booked us a 'quiet room,'" she'd said today, offering her elbow as if to link arms, though in fact they were too mismatched to do so. "All we need is your carriage."

They riveted the museum crowd by strolling side by side to Mr. B.'s office in the third salon, between the waxworks and the mirror hall. The showman was as much an attraction as Anna or the Siamese twins, and when he admitted them, he had to shoo back the crowd.

Vinnie caught Mr. B. up on "old Tom" while one of the office men went to fetch Anna's driver.

They settled back in their seats, waving hand fans while the carriage dodged curious pedestrians, and Vinnie sighed with satisfaction.

Sometimes her friend just needed the bustle of the city, Anna knew.

The Stratton mansion in Bridgeport, with its low doorknobs and miniature furniture, its servants and Thoroughbred horses—and that yacht Charles sailed around the sound in, puffing his cigars—felt too small to Vinnie some days. Anna was proud and pleased to receive her, even if it meant she would have only a short nap (her respite from the heat of July) before tonight's performance.

Once inside, they ordered the full tea service—Lavinia's appetite was enormous, while Anna only picked at her cucumber sandwiches—and got to gabbing right away. As the friends spent more time together—discussing their pasts, their mishaps and mistreatment as entertainers, their impressions of success—they found that they were more alike than not. They found, too, that their lives little resembled the printed biographies Mr. B. sold as souvenirs alongside their cabinet cards in the museum lobby.

The waiter was a stranger today, and tea dribbled from the spout while he tried to keep his eyes on his work and his hands steady on the pot as Lavinia told Anna about her first career as a teacher.

"My height came in handy for darting under students' desks," she said with a wink, "to pinch misbehaving pupils."

Anna almost spit out her tea, to her own mortification, but Vinnie laughed with her as the poor waiter fled the dark-paneled room with a cloth over his arm.

Anna stood and gave her legs a good stretch. She pushed the chair aside, spread her cloth napkin demurely on the floor like a picnic blanket, and eased herself onto it.

"Better?" Vinnie was used to the ritual that brought them eye to eye.

Anna nodded. "I never felt at home in a classroom," she confided. "Long before I was old enough for school, I was too big for the desks." She sipped her tea with her elbow squared, remembering how her father and the brother of the schoolmistress had fitted up a table on planks with a stool tall enough for her legs. At home, she had sat on the floor at mealtimes, as now.

Anna's parents and other good people in New Annan had done their best to make her comfortable in close quarters, but Anna loved to be out under the wide sky best. She loved the meadows and pastures, and to sprawl and read under a tree. She missed those things almost as much as she did Mum and Nanna and the rest of their clan. Mum had managed to stay only a year in the "wicked city," long enough to assess Anna's tutor and establish the rules of Mr. Barnum's patronage.

"Do you ever wonder how your life would be?" she asked. It was easy to imagine Lavinia rapping knuckles in a New England classroom, however glamorous her life was now. "If you had stayed behind to teach?"

"Oh, yes. Every day, I think."

Most etiquette books Anna owned cautioned that direct questions were indelicate, but she pressed on, secure in their friendship. "Do you regret leaving Middleborough, Lavinia?"

"*Vinnie*, darling. I've told you." Her dark eyes softened. "And I don't believe in regret. Meeting Charles was worth leaving home for." She had met her now-husband while working at the museum, and Anna often envied Vinnie her General (or at least what the two of them had together).

Anna had let the resident fortune-teller lure her to her shadowy window at the museum almost as soon as she arrived from Canada. *You dream of love*, Madame Dubois told her, looking up from Anna's giant palm with a bemused air. (Up, and up, and up.) *But I need not say, the odds are . . . steep.* She had leaned closer and lowered her voice. *I can take the pain away*, she vowed. *But it will cost you.*

Anna would have come straight back with another handful of coins had her new friend Isaac the Human Skeleton not explained that Madame's potions were a stew of hog lard and sarsaparilla.

"Stop at twenty-five cents," he advised.

The waiter wheeled in a cart and kept his eyes down while they studied the tea sandwiches. As he served their selections, Anna recalled how very disappointed she had been to learn that the museum's fortune-teller was a fraud. She had cried that night in her room.

Who knew what the future held? There were male giants at the museum, two currently, and Anna had been curious to meet them, having never seen any like herself beyond her reflection in the glass of a shop window.

They were curious, too, perhaps more so. But in the end, Anna rejected their advances.

She was a young lady, and they rebounded like gentlemen, taking a brotherly interest. They even let her enlist them in her learned presentations on the history of their giant race. But it was like herding cats, as Mum used to say, and most days her lectures did without.

"How did you venture from Middleborough to here?" Anna asked Vinnie, watching the waiter roll the cart away and close the velvet curtain, peeking up only once under his lashes.

She was always curious about the other acts at the museum, where they hailed from and how they had suffered, if they had—and they had, almost to the last.

"When I was sixteen, my cousin invited me to work on his Mississippi showboat," Vinnie said. "He was starting up a 'Museum of Living Wonders,' and I knew about the General's success in New York, like everyone else. So I decided to give performing a try. He billed me as the 'Lilliputian Queen.' I sang show tunes and danced a little. I even met another giantess there." She smiled at the memory. "Sylvia Hardy was her name, from Maine. We bunked together and shared a bill sometimes. But her heart wasn't in it and she didn't stay. *I* was the star," Lavinia said. "And you? Did you perform before the museum?"

"Only once. I don't remember it much. I was four and a half feet tall by age four, and strangers took me for a grown woman. They'd see me climbing the hill up from the brook with a pail of water in either hand—or out playing with the others in my mother's coat—and think I was a daftie. When I was five, my father put me on show in Halifax as the 'Infant Giantess.' It was short-lived, I guess, but there was always this question of what to do with me."

Lavinia nodded. "Oh, yes. The *question*."

"At fifteen, I moved to my aunt's in Truro to go to the Normal School—"

"Teachers' college?"

Anna nodded back. "I was over seven feet by then and miserable. People followed me around in the streets. I missed my family so much I felt sick inside. Within a few months, I was back home in New Annan. But when Mr. B. sent his man to ask after me, I told my parents yes."

"But you are the most learned girl I know! And with no schooling?"

"I had tutors, the way I do here." A tutor to further her studies, one who would act as a female attendant or companion, had been key to contract negotiations while Barnum was courting Anna for his museum years ago. She was seventeen when she and her parents traveled to New York. "I hate school," she said, "but I love to learn."

The moment she arrived, Mr. B.'s marvelous museum became Anna's classroom, workplace, and home. The arrangement secured her twenty-three dollars a week in gold, comfortable lodging, and fine clothes, including a spectacular gown of satin (a hundred yards) and lace (fifty yards), costing no less than a thousand dollars. He billed her as "the Tallest Woman in the World." And at eight feet one inch, she surely was, at least with her hair styled for height.

"Imagine if you had *me* for a teacher, Miss Swan. I'd have to stand on tiptoe or a soap box to pinch your knee!"

When their laughter faded, Anna added, "What better teacher could I wish for? The way I look up to you."

Lavinia set her teacup down in the saucer with a loud clink and laughed even harder. "Do you, now?" she teased. "O learned giant!"

Anna laughed, too, but softly. *If you would render yourself pleasing in social parties, never speak to gratify a vanity or passion of your own, but strive to amuse others with themes you know are in accordance with their interests*—and felt herself blush. "I do."

Anna *did* look up to Lavinia, who was older and more worldly, who ordered her jewels from London and wore ermine capes to the theater. Madame Demorest herself, the "goddess of New York fashion," had designed Vinnie's wedding dress, with its two yards of train. It was on display for weeks before the wedding in Madame's shop window. Lavinia was one of the wealthiest women in show business, and while wealth and fame were of less interest to Anna than choice and opportunity, they were, like Vinnie, fine companions.

The sandwiches had been eaten, the teacups drained, and the heat of the day had grown unbearable. They were both visibly perspiring, and Anna still half hoped for that nap before her afternoon lecture, but as the older (not to mention commanding) married lady in the pair, it was Lavinia's prerogative to end their lunch.

Instead, Vinnie leaned forward. The waiter had gone, but chances were good he was eavesdropping behind the curtain. "So. What are people saying about my baby at the museum?"

Taken aback, Anna blinked. "Are you with child?"

A shadow crossed Lavinia's face. "Oh, goodness no. I mean the act."

A year after the Strattons' wedding, Mr. B. had quietly released press photos of Lavinia and her tiny General with a not-tiny baby. Lavinia cradled the child during all public appearances. The public was delighted, as with all developments in the lives of the fairy lovers. The fact that Mr. B. had borrowed the baby from a local orphanage was beside the point. "No ask, no tell," he liked to say.

"A few of us observed," Anna began carefully, "that the baby in the recent pictures did not seem to be the *same* baby."

Lavinia laughed. "The first was outgrowing us. We were about to leave on tour with Minnie and Nutt when it dawned on me. Why haul one infant around when we could send an emissary ahead, choose a baby in each town, and deposit it back at the local orphanage after its star turn? No mess, no expense—beyond Mr. B.'s bountiful donation—no child-care challenges. We had a *slew* of babies. English babies in England, French babies in France, and German babies in Germany."

"Do you and Charles ever think of—?"

"Adopting?" Lavinia cut in, and Anna felt again that heat in her face. Had she overstepped?

Lavinia glanced toward the entryway, where the waiter appeared briefly with a pile of folded napkins. "I worry," she confessed. "Won't the baby be too large?" She winced. "Would it survive? Would *I* survive? Have you never wondered?" she entreated. "Will your body do as it should?"

All the time. Anna wondered about love, marriage, childbirth. And these questions—so ordinary to some—went largely unanswered. Who could she talk to about things so private? *Who will love me? How will I find him?*

She had tried hints and inferences with her adored and outspoken grandmother, but in vain; Nanna was fierce when it came to pride: "Stand tall, lass, and proud." But did she mean proud of Anna the Giantess? Of their Highland ancestry? Of their close-knit Scottish family—Anna was third of what would be thirteen, born to parents of ordinary height—and community?

Thanks to her family and good neighbors, Anna

never suffered the lack of self-worth many of her colleagues at the museum did, the ones "their Annie" wrote home about: the Human Skeleton, dog-faced boys, midgets, dwarfs, and Siamese twins: freaks to the world beyond museum walls; friends to Anna.

But her questions went unanswered. What of the mechanics of a kiss? *Who will reach me — up here?* Only another giant, but Anna knew better than anyone that all things rare are precious. *Who will look inside instead of up?*

She nodded and flipped her fan open, her face ablaze. She was hot. So hot. Anna felt suddenly restless, as if the floor beneath her were on fire. She closed her eyes and rubbed her temples. She would never have that nap now, and her private discomfort threatened to unravel her social graces like thread from a bobbin.

"Are you unwell, dear?"

Anna shook her head but kept her eyes closed.

She tried to concentrate. Here was her chance to ask, to know, and she was too distracted to take it, too timid and too odd. Lavinia was waiting for her reply. "I am sure I worry a great deal," she offered, blinking, and that was all she could bring herself to say.

Lavinia nodded back helpfully. "You never told me how you found Europe, Anna. Queen Victoria received you, yes?"

"Oh, very well." Anna opened her eyes. "I was presented, and . . ." She nodded and blushed, momentarily confused. *Be prudently secret. But don't affect to make a secret of what all the world may know.* "Mr. B. told me Her Majesty was impressed with my 'stateliness and composure.'"

Mr. Barnum had treated Anna like a queen throughout their tour of Great Britain. For eight months they gave receptions in Edinburgh, Glasgow, London, and other cities; Anna couldn't very well visit Scotland without seeing the homes and haunts of her ancestors in Dumfries. Mr. B. indulged these side trips and seemed to enjoy her take on Nanna's stories, the snatches of poetry she remembered well enough to recite on long carriage voyages. Seeing that these green and mysterious places across the ocean were real had changed Anna in some fundamental way, completed her.

Lavinia rested her napkin on the table by her plate and rang the little bell to signal the waiter. "You'll fetch our driver?" she asked him. "He should be at the corner. It's Anna's carriage," she added, gesturing toward her. "You can't miss it."

The waiter bowed and went out with the bill. Vinnie wouldn't let Anna contribute — she never did — and they had little to say on the carriage ride back. They were talked out, and the heat had done them in.

Mr. B. emerged from his office to personally escort Vinnie to her next appointment, waiting while Anna bent — way, way, way down — to offer her friend her cheek. Lavinia kissed it daintily, and they vowed to meet again soon.

Anna exhaled a great breath when they left. She was tired, she realized. There would be just time enough to get to her dressing room, tidy up, and proceed to the big lecture hall, where her talks drew eager crowds.

When she had first arrived at the museum, Mr. B. stationed her in the minor rooms. Anna would stand mute for hours as patrons wandered through and stared, their rude comments leaving her queasy and profoundly homesick, but she had advanced quickly. She was already well-read in the classics when she arrived, with a strong overall knowledge of literature and music. As her studies in piano, voice, and acting progressed, Mr. B. graduated her to the big lecture hall and, right out of the gate, cast her in the role of Lady Macbeth. As her confidence grew by leaps and bounds, Anna began to take pride in her position, in having a career and independence. All the other unmarried young women she knew were domestic servants or factory and mill girls.

This afternoon, as she dressed for her performance and brushed out her hair, Anna replayed her lunch with Lavinia. There were very few conversational topics the friends avoided or found awkward, but today's baby discussion had unsettled her.

Her mind spun from one negative thought to the next, and at last Anna set down her hairbrush, feeling the old burden of being watched without her consent. It wasn't a new sensation. She'd known it all her life, but here at the museum, an otherwise safe space, it took the form of a resident phantom, or the whispered rumor of one, a little child Anna's floor mates claimed to hear late at night in the halls near the menagerie.

Some nights, as she read in her chair by candlelight, her table heaped with novels and histories and the latest issues of *Punch* and *Godey's*, Anna imagined the intruder stationed behind her, craning to read over her elbow. Anna was proud. Proud of her books, her table, the costly new spectacles perched on her nose. She had bought them with her own money. Her carefully outfitted and decorated lodgings were her sanctuary, and she resented any intrusion. Even the suggestion of a lurker reminded her of Truro and the Normal School, of the way strangers had followed her in the streets there, giggling into their hands. The memory of how they had shadowed her, stopped and started as she stopped and started, mocking her every move, may even have influenced her decision to become a performer: she would put herself in charge. She would *permit* them to look at her.

Anna knew well enough that she was marvelous, but there was nothing marvelous about stepping out of a carriage in one swift step while others climbed down. There was nothing curious about an outing to the milliner's: Anna sitting in a chair while the saleslady stood on another to reach her customer's head with a hat.

On Mr. B.'s stage, a female attendant might wrap a

tape measure around Anna's waist while Anna or Mr. Barnum invited a lady volunteer up from the audience. The attendant then wrapped the measure three times around the volunteer's average waist as the audience gasped.

What was mundane to her, Mr. B. had explained, was wondrous to them. Though Anna tried to be accomplished—to be known for what she could do, for what she thought about—the things people delighted in often came at her expense and were painfully embarrassing. As a girl, Anna had paid a call with her mother to the Kents, a respectable family in Tatamagouche. She had entered the house gracefully enough, but when she sat on the end of an antique lounge in their drawing room, the other end tilted perilously up in the air. The littlest Miss Kent had laughed, and Anna had, too, but absently, without joy.

I am so, so tired, she thought, rising to take a last turn before the mirror. For the briefest moment the glass fogged, as from hot breath in the cold, though the room was warm, and Anna thought she saw tiny handprints there.

Who will love me? a little puling voice said. *Who will reach me—up here?*

Anna summoned all her reason.

A mocking ghost would be no more unusual at the museum than any other inmate, she told herself, *and let that be the end of it*. But as she scratched out a few last notes for her lecture about Atlas, the giant who held up the sky, her unease mounted. She huffed and scooped her lecture notes from the table.

It took every ounce of etiquette Anna Swan had not to slam the door.

The "lecture hall" was in fact a large and well-appointed theater with all the trappings — full sets and scenery, footlights, actors, dancers — a venue for plays, melodramas, farce, and pantomime, with two regular performances a day. *Uncle Tom's Cabin*, with the Howard family in the principal roles, was the main-stage sensation of the moment.

Mr. B. billed it a lecture hall to attract respectable patrons who still saw the theater as a place of ill repute. As a respectable young lady herself, Anna, too, preferred the lofty sound of "lecture hall." She took her work seriously, but today's audience was large and unruly and smelled blood, for when Anna lost her train of thought twice running, a man coughed a complaint into his hand, something about the price of admission. As a rule Anna found a clever way to shame a heckler and prevent orange rinds from flying — how easily things got out of hand — but tonight her thoughts were scrambled. She felt singled out, like Atlas, made to bear the weight of the world.

She was fussed all through her talk and hurried upstairs after to fix tea and cool a cloth, laying the damp weight over her eyes as she sank heavily into her chair. She let the arrangement of her rooms and wardrobe, the familiar objects and her pride in them, soothe her, but just as Anna began to settle again, a terrific wail sounded, followed by a thudding and a heavy clatter as of metal bars.

Her apartment was near the menagerie, and within minutes, the wail had built into a cacophony of chirping and prolonged yowling, the metallic clatter building to frenzy.

Anna peeled the damp cloth from her forehead and sat up. Noise was common on this floor. The animals were just down the hall, and on any given day, one captive or another was feeling rough and wild, and some were more vocal than others. But this was different. This was the sound of nightmare, of savage pain and panic.

Beneath the general outcry, Anna heard a violent snarling and hoped the lion hadn't turned on his mate again. The lioness was long-suffering, to say the least, and the mangy Bengal in the facing cage would settle it if she could.

Anna thought to fetch one of the keepers down the hall, but there was already a rhythm of boot heels on the outer staircase.

Uneasy, she stood and crossed to the window. Throngs of people were collecting in front of the building at the corner of Ann Street and Broadway. Many were staring upward, heads bent back on their necks. She waved, but no one seemed to see her.

Anna typically kept her window and heavy curtain closed in the heat. It was cooler that way and muffled noise from the street, but now she tried the latch, and her hand fumbled. When she couldn't jar the window open, she began to panic and rap on the glass. Still, no one seemed to see her. They were busy pointing and gesturing and shouting to others behind them. What were they all looking at? She craned her neck but couldn't make it out at her angle.

Anna sniffed the air as a hard rap sounded on her door, a palm beating the wood. "Anna! Are you in there?"

It was Isaac, and his voice relieved her. "Yes! Here I am," she called back, but her voice fell out like a marble, hard and small. She felt rooted to the spot, though he was pounding harder now, using his hip.

A smell, acrid and half familiar, assaulted her before she heard it, but now that dread word was sounding in every direction, and the bells were clanging. *Fire, fire, fire . . .*

Things happened quickly from there. She half heard the agony of roaring and snarling, the crashing and popping noises, the shrill, darting outcry of monkeys, and something went blank behind her eyes, like those of the old Greek statues. Anna absented herself, as she had learned to do as a child when she was taunted.

The pounding on her door had stopped.

"Isaac?" she said aloud, and then, hysterically: *"Isaac!"*

She slid down the wall and huddled over her knees while smoke curled under the door from the hall.

What seemed an eternity later, someone — not Isaac, who was too slight for such a task — kicked open her door, and flame leaped behind and around him as she gasped. He beat it back with a wet wool blanket he'd secured, holding out a hand to her. "Come, now, Miss Swan. It's fine. Take my hand."

But he was too far away, and other men, shadows swinging axes in the fiery hall, were shouting that the stairs were alight and would not hold her. The man at the door and another she didn't recognize were both calling to her now, as if she were a cat under a carriage. When she didn't respond, they ran over and tried to heave her to her feet, each grasping a wrist hard, but she sat leaden, yanking her hands back and rubbing the hurt wrists. She closed her eyes and hummed and shrank back against the wall.

"I tell you," another man called in, "don't bother! The stairs won't hold her! They're ready to collapse. We're going down."

The man from the door told his companion, "Get the window open. . . . Call down for a ladder!"

"She'll never go through. . . ."

"She'll have to! She's had a shock. Shake her!"

The man by the window kept looking at the stairs, which now glowed as orange as coals when you blow on them, but he obeyed, breaking the latch with his ax handle and prying the window up. "I mean she won't *fit!*" His eyes were wild. "Look at the size of her."

Anna was used to other people discoursing about her "circumstances" in her presence, as if she were not there. It had been so all her life, though as she matured, her parents learned to respect her enough to meet her eyes and include her in such discussions.

As the man forced the window open, the flames in the hall spiked and rolled into the room in a truly terrifying way, sinking back again as a battalion of shrieking monkeys—monkeys of every size and shape and color—came swinging overhead, hand over deft hand, bouncing off the walls of Anna's drawing room on their heels and knocking over all and sundry on their way out. One by one, they sailed through the open window, some headed toward the roof and others down a drain spout into the packed street, where a few humans gave chase.

Anna saw the fugitives vanish into the crowd as you see impossible things in dreams.

Her rescuers were calling to other men in the street, men propping up ladders too small to support a giant. Workmen from the museum had found a derrick nearby, and the crowd parted to let them through with it, flowing together again like water.

While the men worked, Anna watched the chaos in the hall. She saw blistered snakes coiled on the banister, dropping and writhing down the glowing staircase. She saw a tide of steaming water — dirty salt water from the North River, she knew — pouring from the room where the great tank was. Anna couldn't ponder the fate of the beautiful white whales — the thought was an abyss that threatened her remove. She fixed her eyes and mind instead on a singed cat padding past the door. It would escape, she thought pitifully. It *could* escape.

What will become of you? she thought coolly as raging flames circled her sanctuary. Everything she had earned and built for herself with her outsize hands, with her voice and mind and heart, would soon be gone. This she knew as she knew her own name.

Anna was not inclined to self-pity but couldn't stop the tears streaking her round cheeks. The smoke and the smell and the shouting were too much, and just when she thought she might faint dead away and be done with it, ax blades split the walls around the window with hard strokes. *One, two, three, four.* Two of her champions had made use of the ladders and were hacking their way to her.

If she could rally, she might fetch that locked box yet — her whole life's savings, $1,200 in gold — from its hidey-hole in the closet. She might secure her future if only she could move, but her limbs felt thick and slow as molasses, and the men outside were gesturing like madmen in a dream. *Move. Step here. Do this. Fly. You will fly, Miss Swan.*

But fly where? The museum *was* her home now. Who was she without it?

One wide step and another, a shifting of skirts and petticoats, a sickening sway as they helped her balance, all 394 pounds of her.

They lowered Anna, who clutched and winced and strained every muscle to hold on, by block and tackle, eighteen men grasping the end of the rope. She sailed and swayed over the sea of hats in the street, yet another audience, a uniform mass applauding with joy, it seemed, such joy — as much because some kind soul had released the birds from the aviary upstairs, and almost as one they burst from a corresponding window, a wheeling, feathered blur: parrots, cockatoos, mockingbirds, hummingbirds, vultures, and eagles, even the great, stiff, clumsy condor. The crowd in the street seemed to sway with them as they flapped free, and for the instant Anna floated on air as her rescue crew paused to take in the sight, and for the merest instant she felt it, too, swaying there, the beauty of the moment.

They had her carriage waiting for her by the curb, and Anna was rushed to the Metropolitan Hotel, a matron riding along as chaperone to hold her sooty hands and dab at her eyes with a handkerchief smelling of lavender (ever after, Anna would smell lavender on her mother's linens and think of sorrow).

Arriving in the lobby, Anna wanted so much to sleep but was afraid to go to her room, afraid to dream, to be alone, so when the matron left her, she sat by the street-facing window, shivering in the heat, watching the flow of pedestrian traffic hurrying in the direction of the doomed museum.

When her colleagues found her and couldn't coax her to go up and rest, the maître d' admitted her — quite against the rules, after a rousing poll — into the men's smoking room, which was mostly abuzz with exiled museum employees at the moment.

The comic singer, Mr. Harrison, was in the middle of a funny story, the "annals of his escape." He was in his dressing room, he said, when he heard the hullabaloo on Broadway and, taking to the window, deduced what was going on and rushed to the stage. The auditorium was filled with smoke from a fire in the engine room, someone notified him, spouting the party line that it would soon be out. Mr. Harrison thought better of it and returned for his wardrobe. The smoke was so dense beneath the stage that he had trouble locating his dressing room, but he managed to snatch up his character wigs and cash box, resolving to leave the building.

Their colleagues in the theatrical department were throwing dramatic costumes and other valuables out the windows into the street as he passed, most of which were trampled or seized by the public.

"Nice try, gentlemen!" he called now, raising his glass. The others raised theirs in turn.

When he reached the main saloon where the wax figures stood, Harrison went on, he found a scene of great confusion. The public was swarming, trying to rescue (or more likely make off with) the valuable wax figures—Napoleon with his squint, Queen Victoria, Tom Thumb and family—through the billiard room, but Barnum's office was on the same floor. He emerged in a fury, shouting that the duration of the fire would not be long, but his memory would be. "I will not suffer thieves!" All through his scolding, people rushed for the front windows and emptied their arms blindly onto the curb. A fireman made coolly for the street with Franklin Pierce under one arm and the Veiled Murderess under the other.

No one had yet broken the glass case across the room to appropriate Christ and His Disciples, though Mr. Harrison did watch a fellow make off with the effigy of Jefferson Davis. This led to a spin-off tale that Anna had never heard. The ousted Confederate president had worn his wife's dress to escape arrest but was captured anyway. Good old Mr. B. had tried and failed to obtain the original petticoats Davis wore, so commissioned a wax figure of the fallen leader incognito, presenting it at the museum as the "Belle of Richmond."

This inspired a swell of laughter and more clinking of glasses and mugs, until someone put in, "I trust the others melted down to the floor."

"They *were* perspiring a bit," Mr. Harrison said, trying to keep things light, but a melancholy had seeped in. There were sighs all around.

"They're made of fat, after all," someone added. "They must've fed the fire."

"All but the pink lady!" Mr. Harrison thundered, swallowing more ale.

He had assumed a mission to keep spirits high, Anna saw. Those who had not heard the tale now begged for it. "As I was leaving the building, a cry went up at Falcon and Vesey Streets that a woman was being saved from the blaze," Mr. Harrison began in his tremulous and expressive voice, which seemed always on the verge of breaking into song. "The crowd was on tiptoe to learn who the lady was and by what means she was being dispatched from a hideous death. And they didn't have long to wait, for this vision in pink soon appeared above, where she was being handed down from story to story by the gallant folk inside. Through the cheers, it became clear that the maiden was not fair and not a lady, but another wax figure. The deception roused the crowd, who were as merry as they were mean."

"Wasn't that when someone shouted, 'The snakes are loose!'?"

"Yes," others put in eagerly, "and that explosion . . ."

Anna remembered it, though it came out that it was no explosion but the whistling of a steam fire engine somewhere around Vesey and Broadway. The noise sent hundreds scampering, shoving, and scaling the towering iron gate into St. Paul's churchyard. Scores made it all the way to the river before daring to look back. Hats, canes, and watches went missing, coats were torn and ankles twisted, and not a few suffered a good roll in the mud or a trample.

"As for those hats!" Mr. Harrison chimed in again, inspiring a wave of nervous laughter.

"After the blast," a man told Anna, leaning toward her when he saw the question on her face, "boys were marauding around with half a dozen hats each stacked on their heads."

"Speaking of hats," another man said, "Knox lost a fair deal of stock, too. The crowd cleaned him out of Panama hats before the rush was over. And I heard two fellas dressed as soldiers got nabbed each with a dozen pairs of shoes under his coat."

Anna had a strange memory of a handsome fireman emerging from the building with a stuffed owl in his hands.

"Who knows how it started?"

A defective furnace in the cellar under Groop's restaurant was the consensus. The furnace was beneath the office of the museum, at number 8 Ann Street, and the alarm had sounded immediately. *An hour earlier*, Anna thought, and the thought chilled her, *the alarm would have triggered panic in her surly audience, leading to a stampede.* A great many lives might have been lost.

One man wondered aloud if the fire were sabotage — set purposefully by those who resented Barnum's presence on the Connecticut legislature, where he had been a vocal supporter of abolition.

"Southern sympathizers?"

None felt qualified to comment, though many dropped their eyes. It was a terrible thought, on many levels.

Now a new group entered, faces sooty. Anna recognized one of the animal keepers, red eyed and sickly pale. Another man removed his streaked seersucker jacket. "I left after the roof collapsed. Couldn't bear to look anymore." He caught his breath a moment. "The place looked like the crater of a volcano."

Another described how, around 1:30, the wall on the Ann Street side of the museum had fallen with a noise like a powder magazine exploding. The huge cloud of dust and smoke had made it look like dusk at midday.

By 1:45, the Broadway front had collapsed in three sections, one swiftly after another. The great facade wavered and whistled forward, falling not flat into the burning ruins but out onto Broadway. It smashed on the pavement with a spray of smoke, bricks, and mortar, "and that," said the keeper of countless dead charges, from mammoth whales to the rarest little bird, "was the end of the old museum."

The only curiosities saved for posterity, he said, or for Barnum's benefit (besides the pink lady, now in police custody), were Ned the "learned seal" and a case of rare coins.

There was a moment of silent reflection. After a rash of weary yawns, Mr. Harrison led a final toast. "And here's to the courageous living curiosity in our midst. Long may she reign." Mugs were raised in Anna's honor, and she blushed. *You will please so much the less, if you go into company determined to shine. Let your conversation appear to rise out of thoughts suggested by the occasion. . . .*

As she hunched in a wool blanket, safe in a circle of cigar smoke and sadly smiling faces, Anna sipped her brandy, feeling worldly and tragic. It was a new but not entirely strange sensation. The show was not over yet.

THE BEARDED
LADY'S SON

It was the growing conviction that something
was stealthily following him which tried the
nerves of Bob Marshall, for it is the unseen
that tests one's bravery.

— P. T. Barnum, *The Wild Beasts,
Birds and Reptiles of the World:
The Story of Their Capture*

Here was the shame of it. He was sixteen, and his mother had a beard, and he didn't.

When they lived in Jersey, the carnies had teased him mercilessly about it, though he'd also lied about his age to get work. Now his mother's beard was making his dreams come true.

It wasn't until they were moved into their spacious room in the new American Museum, with Jack bunked on the sofa as usual and Ma cheerily unwrapping dishes and stowing them in the cabinet over the little stove, that he got the bad news.

"There's one thing, love . . . about"—she waved— "all this."

"What's that?" He unwound his pen-and-ink set from the paper she'd packed it in. Jack wouldn't be able to sleep tonight, so he'd clean the nibs and sketch a while when she turned in for the night. There was no better inspiration than insomnia. The silence finally made him look up. "Ma?"

"No one can know about you." She kept her back to him.

"Know about me?"

"That I have . . . a child."

"Ma, you're talking to the wall," he said, "and . . . I'm not a child."

"Of course you're not." She swiveled, a delicate look on her face. "But you don't have a father, and I'm not married, and that makes you—"

"A *bastard*." It was a word they never spoke, a forbidden word. She would sooner sew his mouth shut, she had once said, than hear him speak the word.

"Illegitimate," she reminded him, and he could see that his vulgarity had wounded her, the way he'd spat the word out like a pit.

Her beard looked exceptionally dark right now, dark as those shriveled olives in the deli. It looked hideous, and he wanted to pull it. He wanted to make her turn her face away. "Stop looking at me," he said.

"Jack, listen."

"Don't *look at me!*" He turned away, as she had done, only not out of cowardice.

Despair.

"You are illegitimate," she went on softly, touching his slumping shoulder, "and so . . . through no fault of our own, we aren't respectable. Mr. Barnum runs a respectable establishment."

She touched his shoulder again, and he flinched. "I could lose this job, Jack. Didn't you want me to work here?"

I wanted us *to work here.*

From the time he was eleven or twelve, Jack had always talked his way into a job at whatever operation hired Ma. She kept a low profile, then as now, showing up only for her assigned time in the sideshow tent, but he would do just about any work to be around the animals. Jack would muck stalls, spread feed for chickens, groom ponies kids rode in circles when the carousel was broken, which no matter where they worked it mostly was.

Jack had a way with animals. He'd ask for a week to prove himself, and he always did, but it was Ma the promoters wanted—a bearded lady with at least one fine dress—someone for people to gawp at alongside pinheads, fire eaters, and four-legged girls. Jack had just been along for the ride.

She walked to one of the unpacked crates, fetched an old metal biscuit can, and fished out a newspaper clipping. Ma unfolded the yellowing paper and held it under his chin, her hand with its hairy knuckles trembling to keep it there. It was a letter to the editor dated long before he was born.

She set it down on the table where he could see it if he chose. "I cut it out when I entered puberty and the hair wouldn't stop growing. His museum seemed like a place I might like to work one day . . . a *safe* place."

He waited for her to go on, but she didn't.

Jack sat up and skimmed the letter:

Dear Sir:

—A friend has just handed me your paper of Friday last in which is detailed an account of a

most rascally and impudent attempt on the part
of some male visitor to the Museum, to engage
in an improper familiarity with a young lady
from your city. . . . I am deeply grieved to learn
that such a transaction should have occurred
here. . . . The "rules and regulations" of the
Museum are publicly placarded throughout the
building, and they contain the following paragraph: *As the manager is particularly desirous of
maintaining good order and propriety throughout the
establishment, he will regard as a favor, the report to
his office of any improper conduct on the part of visitors or employees of the Museum.* I most deeply
regret . . . My intention ever has been, and shall
be, to preserve at all times the most rigid decorum and propriety throughout the museum, so
that parents and husbands may feel . . . I keep
men stationed in each hall of the Museum, and
no public breach of decorum could possibly
escape their scrutiny . . .

Respectfully yours,

P. T. Barnum, Manager of the Am. Museum

She tried to touch his shoulder again, but he
flinched. "Do you understand, Jack?"

Oh, he understood. *It's why she waited so long. It's why
she suffered in terrible curtained rooms,* he thought, *where
lewd men yanked her beard, where ladies sneered and poked her*

with parasols, night after night, year after year ... when she could have been a star in Barnum's crown, when she could have worn Napoleon's diamonds.

When they first moved to the city to find his mother a new promoter and hopefully a spot in a dime museum, Ma had been frightened and intimidated. She kept her curtains closed to the crime and mess of the tenements, and when they rode the stage uptown, she felt even worse. All those people with their fancy clothes and cultured airs only reminded her, she said, how little she had to give him.

In the "day world," Ma wore black and a veil so people thought she was in mourning, and maybe she was, at least when they'd arrived in New York. Maybe always, like that queen in England after her prince died. Ma never seemed happy. Jack more than anyone had tried to make her happy, and he knew she loved him: she told him so all the time, stroking his right eyebrow — always the right — or picking the straw from his hair.

She would smile her slanting smile and look a world away from mannish, but it didn't make her as happy as it made him: to Jack, Ma's smile was like catching a fish with your bare hands.

Here in New York, "happy" had seemed beyond Ma's reach. He would come home and find her in the floral chair with the sharp springs, just staring out their top-floor window at the fading sky — so still, he'd want to shake her. He'd beg her to light a candle, cook some dinner, look alive. Sometimes he'd wave a hand in front of her hairy mug. Not one muscle in her face would move, but her amber eyes rolled up toward him, so sad. What kind of world put that look in Ma's eyes?

It had been his idea for her to contact Mr. Barnum, the world's greatest showman, who, as it happened, was right here in Manhattan. He had reopened his American Museum two years after a tragic fire destroyed the first.

Ma objected to the idea. She wasn't "special enough," she said — no Josephine Clofullia.

The Swiss Bearded Lady had toured all over Europe as a young woman. She got a huge diamond from Napoleon III after styling her beard after his. In time, she moved to America with her husband and son to work for Mr. Barnum, who officially recorded her beard at six inches.

Madame Clofullia dressed very fine and was known for scolding rowdy patrons: "I am a lady. I beg you not to forget that." She would show off the brooch pinned to her dress with its cameo of her husband, Monsieur Fortune Clofullia, who was bearded, too. So was their son, Albert. Barnum named him "Infant Esau," after the figure in the Bible.

Jack wished Ma had half of Madame Clofullia's nerve and confidence. He could be her manager, and they'd get rich and buy a big menagerie, and Jack would sit and draw animals all day with the pen and ink she gave him for his sixteenth birthday.

Six months passed, and Ma worked in some terrible places. Jack knew they were terrible only because she told him so. She refused to let him find a job in New York until she got "her bearings." He was too young, she kept saying, which was absurd, since every newsie and factory boy was younger than Jack.

It was a terrible world, she said, and he was too "good." She would not see him out all alone in it.

"Jack?" she tried now.

He refused to turn around. He had to catch his breath. He had to think. There was always a way, Jack believed. He was an optimist.

He looked up at her quickly. "Can't we say I *had* a father, and he died?"

"That would be a lie, Jack. You know I don't lie. I've never lied to you."

"Never?"

"Never. You know how Mr. Geppetto made Pinocchio's nose grow if he told a lie? If I tell one, my beard grows. It would be down to the floor if I learned to lie to you."

"Mr. Barnum would give you a raise." He smiled, or tried to. Jack liked his stupid jokes. When Ma joked or smiled, it was like a holiday.

"We'll figure it out," he told his mother, who looked younger than she had in months. Who looked . . . happy.

Ma did not lie to him, but that didn't stop Jack from lying to her.

The moment she left to perform for the day, he poked his head out the door of their apartment, peered up and down the hall, and slipped out with a little stool under his arm and his pen-and-ink kit bundled in news sheet and stuffed in a pocket, closing the door behind him.

It was easy enough blend in with the animals. All he had to do was park his stool in the mob of museum visitors, let them hide him, or find a quiet nook beside a cage. He concealed himself reasonably well and went to work, shifting his stool here and there as needed for each sketch.

One Monday morning, when the menagerie was deserted but for Jack and the animals, or seemed to be — he was in that place of deep concentration that made the world go away — a voice startled him, and he dropped his pen. The ink pot was on the floor, and he shifted it carefully to the side so it didn't brush the lady's hem.

"That's a fine likeness."

The voice belonged to a very pregnant woman in a fine blue dress. She was standing barely two feet away, with one hand on her lower back, supporting herself, it seemed. Her chestnut hair was loose from its pins in front. She had pretty hazel eyes and fanned herself with her silk hat.

"Thank you kindly, ma'am." He dipped his head in a little bow and averted his eyes. Then he thought to jump up and offer her his stool.

"Oh, no." She lifted a hand as if to stop him. "Thanks but no. I need to walk it off."

Jack sat back down, uncertain if she meant the baby or a backache, but it wouldn't be polite to inquire either way, or even reply. Ladies never spoke to him, besides his mother, much less grown ladies in fine silk with babies on the way, much less about his pictures.

"I'm especially impressed with that," she said, stabbing a slender finger to the crosshatching on Henry's face. The nail on her index finger clicked against the book he was using for a desk. The "desk" was propped on his thighs, which made his face burn still more than before.

"You got her mug just right," she said. "She's a terrible ham with those shifty eyes. The expression's perfect."

Her mug. So Henry was a girl. Jack blushed and felt a terrible urge to cover his sketch. He was proud of it. He could draw bears like nobody's business, but he didn't feel ready to show his work to anyone besides Ma. He didn't know if his pictures were good or if they just seemed to be good because they were his and because he lavished so much time and attention on them.

"I come in before the crowds," she said. "I've seen you before . . . drawing them."

Jack thought of Mr. Barnum's letter to the editor and the museum guards and wondered if he should politely excuse himself. He didn't want her to think he was being too familiar. He didn't want to be collared and exposed. He didn't want to ruin Ma's life again.

"Every time I'm in New York, I come in and look for my cat," the lady said absently, as if she were talking to herself.

There were no cats in the menagerie, Jack thought, unless you counted the lions, and he wondered if she might be talking about the fire.

He and Ma still lived in Jersey then, but Jack had read all about the destruction of the first museum, the great fire the giant girl had been rescued from, in the evening editions.

One reporter—Jack couldn't remember for which paper—happened to be stationed at a window in a building across the street during the blaze, a window overlooking one in the menagerie where the museum's wild animals lived. The reporter had watched those captives die, each and every one apart from the scattering of monkeys and birds who escaped through windows. The reporter witnessed it all and wrote about it in excruciating detail. His article was the worst sort of sensationalism, Ma said, but unlike some other readers, maybe, Jack felt and believed every word.

The fire raged in his dreams for days and weeks afterward. The sounds, sights, and smells felt to him more like memories than dreams, as if he had really been there, really seen the way the lion and his mate hurled themselves against the bars time and again until the grate gave way and tipped with a crash. The cats had leaped down and hunched a long moment with their tails lashing, stunned by liberty. He saw, too, the way the top of the three-tiered cage fell forward in flames, its rods dropping to the floor, crushing some creatures and freeing others that limped or scurried or dashed off to fiery deaths in other parts of the building.

Jack heard the crash and snarling when the tiger and the polar bear forced open their enclosures, watched snakes flip and blister, smelled singeing fur and flesh, and glimpsed a savage tangle of lion and tiger tipping straight into the blaze. From time to time, the flames rolled back into the hall, and the smoke cleared, revealing monkeys perched on high and shivering with dread, afraid to leap out the windows until the fire belched again, shooting white-hot light and smoke into the room. Worst of all, Jack saw in his mind's eye the end of the beautiful white whales from Labrador. Alongside the alligators, they had writhed in boiling water until firemen cracked the glass of their tanks, hoping to drench the room, when the great beasts rolled out in a rush of steaming water to shudder and die on the floor.

Was it true? Or was it puffery, as Ma claimed, a way to sell papers? Jack hoped it *was* just a story, a hoax, but he replayed every paragraph of the reporter's eyewitness account in his mind until he'd memorized it like a poem. It had been that real to him.

It was real to him now, three years later, the fear and fury those trapped animals must have felt at their end.

The new captives were his classroom and his teachers. He liked to see them behave, predict their actions at feeding time, their scuffling for territory. He was learning to draw the animals quickly, to mimic the drama, the poses he'd seen in engravings in magazines.

"Her name was Clementine," the lady said, and Jack must have misheard, for he blurted out, "I'm Jack."

"Oh, no." She laughed. "*I'm* Helen. But hi, Jack." She held out her gloved hand, and since he didn't know what else to do, he shook it, mortified.

"The *cat* was Clementine. Mother sent her to live at the museum, and I never saw her again. She was about as big as I am now, ready to birth her kittens."

There were cats, Jack remembered, in the Happy Family display upstairs. It featured all manner of small animals — predator and prey, the placard boasted, trained to live in harmony (Jack had seen a thing or two and begged to differ) — from owls to monkeys.

"Daddy promised he delivered her. He teased me they fed her to the lions like keepers at the London Menagerie used to do; you could buy your ticket that way — by handing over your pet. I know he wouldn't do any such thing, but he might have shaken her out of her basket into the street. Clem was a wild one and could fend for herself, but she had those babies on the way." Helen gazed around wistfully. Henry had stopped pacing, almost as if he were listening. "I expect she's long gone now."

"What did she look like?" Jack asked, trying to be kind. "I'll keep an eye out."

"Oh, she'd be ancient now." Helen suddenly looked as sad as Ma on a bad day. He noticed the dark circles under her hazel eyes. He couldn't tell how old she was, only that she felt older. "I never forgave my mother for that." She looked over at him, as if he would understand (and maybe he did — he was none too pleased with his own mother right now).

They stood in congenial silence a while as Henry groomed his right shoulder, nibbling on whatever it was he found.

"You draw well." Helen held out her hand expectantly. "May I see the others?"

He let her take the pages from his grasp and flip through, smiling. She nodded and returned Henry to the top. The ink had dried, luckily.

"Very lifelike," she said. "I wish you'd show my father. These should be in books."

Jack had never thought of books. He sometimes imagined his drawings hanging on walls in gilded frames, but never decorating a page.

Their second day in New York, Ma had come home

with what she called a "big book of substance." She'd spent half their savings, Jack supposed, to buy him the tale of a mad captain bent on chasing a whale "round perdition's flames" until he speared it. Jack had never read a book like it. The illustrations had riveted him, and "perdition's flames" became his favorite phrase, though it also made him think of the museum, and the fire. Jack would never view a whale the same way again.

But he had Ma to thank for a steady supply of books. They didn't have the money to spare on luxuries, so when she insisted, he'd ask for dime novels, *Beadle's Weekly*, that sort of thing. He liked Wild West yarns, but it was the animal stories that got him through the long, dull days when he wasn't working.

Jack wanted so much to let the words slip out — *your father?* — but Helen was nothing if not forthcoming. He supposed she would tell him if she meant to.

When she went quiet, walking back and forth along with Henry and cooing at him, Jack said impulsively, "He lets you come in here alone? Your father?" He knew he was out of line, but curiosity had the better of him. It *was* a dirty place and a loud one, and the smell was hard to stomach sometimes. "A fine lady like you?"

"Oh, he can't stop me," she said, smiling. "I think of them as mine . . . the animals."

I do, too.

"And I'm not so much a lady," she added. "Anyone will tell you. He'll be the first. My father."

Jack thought of her as "Lady Helen" after that.

Lady Helen smiled and walked away, and as she turned the corner, he called, "Don't worry about Clementine." She paused, the edge of her dress just visible on the stone floor. "There are always plenty of mice in here."

He meant it to be consoling, and maybe it was, but he'd never know. The trace of blue dress was gone.

As always, Jack kept a close eye on the old pocket watch that had once belonged to his father, to make it back before Ma. He meant to start dinner but took out his pen and got down to the fine work on today's pictures, crosshatching shadows and adding ferns and landscapes from his imagination.

At some point he paused to heat water for potatoes, sat down again, and started rolling his pen back and forth across the tabletop. Did she expect him to stay in this room forever?

Why does it matter what I do?

Wasn't he the man of the house?

And why did *she* get to be happy when he didn't?

Jack set down his pen and began to pace, like Henry in the cage downstairs.

Does she hope I'll go away?

He was old enough now, Jack supposed. Ma had left home at sixteen.

He would never be an infant Esau, no matter how

he tried; Jack's chin stayed smooth as a baby's behind no matter how much meat he ate, and there were no signs of fuzz blooming anytime soon. But he had no trouble imagining himself as more hirsute than Ma, a right dog-faced boy, or better yet covered entirely in fur like one of the animals in the menagerie, like Henry, who smelled of musk and orange peel.

But he would rather just draw them.

And why shouldn't he? Jack thought of Lady Helen perusing his pages and smiled.

When the alarm sounded, he woke on the sofa with a jolt.

Ma had come home and rescued the potatoes while he was asleep — and must have heard it first. She had already scurried from behind the screen in her dressing gown and untied boots, her best dress under an arm. She extended her hand and heaved him up. "Coat and shoes," she commanded, trying to catch his wrist when he turned back for his pens and drawings instead, but he broke away and scooped them up.

She pushed him roughly out to the hall and into the stream of people bumping their way down the steps.

One staircase, two, three — they moved like sleep-walkers, some with damp cloths pressed to their mouths. They spilled out into the bitter cold in various states of undress, most draped in wool or calico blankets.

Smoke from the lower level, where the boilers and machinery and the menagerie were, was rising all around, and when Jack tried to go back, shouting about the animals, two burly stage men hooked him under his armpits to hold him. They nearly lifted him, kicking, off the curb. "They can't be saved now," one said. The other tightened his grip when Jack elbowed him to get free. "*Look,* boy." He pointed with his chin. Already, the main entrance was the yawning mouth of a dragon, belching fire.

The clamor and yowling from below, more pitiful now than agonized, had started up again—Jack realized he had been hearing it all along and not registering it, not until Ma clapped her hands over his ears as they were climbing the steps of the tavern across the street. One of his captors now had an arm locked around his throat in an awkward embrace, and with Ma's cold palms pressed to his ears, trying to drown out the cries, the party moved almost as one form, some lurching beast, up the tavern steps. Everyone from the museum was pouring into the hearth room to wait for news while the barman dispensed whiskey.

Always a fan of innovative new technology, Mr. Barnum used little-tested boilers to heat the new building. It was a frigid March night, with the machines working overtime, and just after midnight, a flue malfunctioned. The local firemen were on a call and took an hour to reach the museum, and when they did, the water from their hoses froze solid on the building's granite facade.

In the morning, that front, draped in icicles, was the only thing standing.

Many museum residents, like Ma, needed to find accommodations and stayed on at the tavern for days at Mr. Barnum's expense; they were on hand when the showman arrived to console his evacuees and inspect the ruins.

Jack and Ma were sharing a bowl of stew near the hearth when Mr. Barnum opened the door and let in a gust. But it wasn't Mr. Barnum who caught Jack's eye. It was the lady in the fine carriage behind him. He put his napkin down and excused himself. He had wondered if he would ever see her again, and whether she had had her baby, and whether her baby would be a boy or a girl. He ambled over, opened the tavern door, and closed it behind him. Now what? He stood a moment, moving from foot to foot and blowing on his hands, not because he didn't know how to address a gentlewoman in a fine carriage, Mr. Barnum's fine carriage, but because he could see her face through the frosted glass. Her chestnut hair was tightly coiled today, piled under a stylish hat, not loose in front, and while her head was bowed, he could see that she was crying, openly weeping. She didn't notice him standing out there at first, staring up at her like a fool, his breath a wind of ice.

She recognized him eventually, though, and

motioned him over in that forward way of hers, and he lifted a finger as if to say *Wait one minute*. He walked back inside, where Mr. Barnum had accepted a mug of steaming hot chocolate. He was holding court by the bar, comforting and being comforted. He happened to look up when Jack came in and returned to the table.

Mr. Barnum nodded right at him, then looked at Ma and back at Jack. Ma smiled faintly. How could it matter now? That she had a son, or that her son might be a bastard? Jack snatched his drawings from the table, and she knew enough to let him be.

Jack walked over to the bar and blurted, "The animals, sir —" but Mr. Barnum, already deep in another conversation, shook his head and lifted a hand as if to plead *Not now*, and perhaps, *but one day we'll speak of it.*

Jack ran outside, and Helen opened the carriage to him. She smeared her tear tracks with gloved fingers. He couldn't speak, words wouldn't come, but he thrust the pages at her and then lurched on past. He ran. Jack ran and ran, for what seemed half the night. He slept in a doorway and nearly froze. But he didn't.

Before they boarded the train to Aunt Sue's in Jersey later that week, Jack jogged across to the museum for a last look at the ruins.

Men were still chopping at the ice and charred brick with picks and axes, breathing frost, rubbing their raw hands together. There wasn't much to salvage. A contractor combing through tipped his hat when Jack greeted him, and confirmed the rumors. The animals were all lost. "Just like the first time." The man's scarred face brightened. "'Cept Mabel."

"Mabel?"

"The bear. Not the white one —"

Henry!

Jack grabbed the startled man's hand and pumped it up and down. It was as cold as ice. He felt for his pens in his pocket and jogged back, slipping on the ice, to catch his train.

IT'S NOT HUMBUG IF YOU BELIEVE IT

I don't believe in duping the public, but I believe
in first attracting and then pleasing them.
— P. T. Barnum

Diana slipped into the booth, breathless.

"You're late," Pauline complained. It was bad enough that they didn't believe her ... didn't believe Daddy. "What did Cliff say?"

"He agrees. It's humbug. Just as Mr. B. said." She nodded at Pauline and pronounced, "There *are* no spirits."

All three paused to let that soak that in.

Pauline turned and petted their other friend's silken back in circles — little, tentative baby strokes, as if Lillian might fly to pieces if jostled.

"Cliff said he sold Mr. Mumler some backdrops just last month and delivered them himself. He had a good look at his operation before the sting." Both Diana and Pauline were fond of theatrical words like *operation* and *sting*. "He said they'll arrest him soon and rule guilty. They'll shut him up in prison for a long time. At the very least, they'll board up his studio. So we'd better go through with it, Lil, if we're going to. I made the appointment weeks ago, and he hasn't canceled it."

Lillian had teared up again, so Pauline bit her tongue. *Let's go!* was on the tip of it. *What are we waiting for?*

Though it took an inordinately long time for Lil to learn of it (and she hadn't mentioned Jeremiah in all the years Pauline had known her), Lil's first love, Jeremiah from Pennsylvania, had died at Gettysburg. Ages ago, of course, and the war was over, but a dead beau was as good an excuse as any to visit a notorious criminal's photography studio and have their portraits taken with spirits. There was one complication. Daddy.

There had been developments since Diana had Cliff make their appointment. Mr. Mumler, the photographer, was on the verge of being arrested. Rumor was there would be a trial, and if there was, P. T. Barnum of the American Museum had volunteered his services.

If charges were brought against the notorious spirit photographer, Daddy would be a star witness.

"I told you it was rot," Pauline said, triumphant. This was a doomed outing (not to mention expensive — Mr. Mumler charged a fortune for his portraits, which were inferior, Cliff said, from an artistic point of view), and Pauline was proud of her father, even if he did rain on everyone else's parade while his own marched merrily onward.

That said, it was all the rage to have a portrait done by Mr. Mumler, and why should Pauline not have one while she still could? Pauline couldn't imagine which spirit might visit her — some old trickster from the Barnum clan, probably, who'd thumb his red nose behind her back.

Daddy hated the Spiritualists but admired their sense of spectacle. He knew all the tricks, and over meals at the country house regaled Pauline and her long-suffering mother with the mechanics of séance manifestations. He was excited about the trial, he had said at that morning's breakfast, sipping his cocoa. "I'll enjoy it."

"*Is* there a trial?" Pauline asked him innocently.

"No, but there will be. They'll shut him down and lock him in the Tombs."

"But why?" Pauline asked, less innocently. "Don't *you* fool people for a living?"

What right did Daddy have to testify against Mr. Mumler when what he did every day, what he'd always done, was so much worse by the same standards?

"The difference," he said, "as narrated at great length in a familiar exposé by yours truly, is criminal misrepresentation. Don't you read my books, Sweet P.?"

She smacked a hand over her mouth. *Of course!* "Mr. *Mumler* was the spirit photographer in your book?" She was stunned and ashamed. Caroline had always been the one to keep track of Daddy's many accomplishments, and Helen was the reader. But now she remembered. In his book on humbug, with its ponderous subtitle — *An Account of Humbugs, Delusions, Impositions, Quackeries, Deceits and Deceivers Generally, in All Ages* — Daddy had introduced "an ingenious man and scientific chemist" who fooled his clients by pretending to take portraits of them with their dead loved ones. He had purchased spirit photographs from the gentleman, years ago, for the museum. But it struck him that taking advantage of bereaved people with trick pictures was a very different brand of humbug from harmless hoaxes that gave pleasure. "I call it entertainment," he told Pauline now. "Mumler calls it truth."

Pauline didn't press her point, though she might have. It was allowance day, and she needed money to pay Mr. Mumler. The last thing she wanted was to offend her father.

She for one was happy to be fooled if it amused her. Pauline was fond of amusement and excitement and all things nefarious—and she was not inclined to be skeptical. Truth for truth's sake was dull. Things only got interesting when people made assumptions.

Pauline and her friends were fashionable and artistic, and Diana's fiancé, Cliff, was in vogue at the moment as a painter and sculptor catering to photographers. His backgrounds of snowy city streets and Moorish ruins, and the papier-mâché columns, balustrades, and rocks he sculpted, were in great demand by famous portrait photographers for their studios and also used for fancy-dress balls and *tableaux vivants*.

The new studio trend, Cliff had explained, was to use props like his to pose sitters more naturally. No more fitting a subject's head into a cold clamp (to Pauline, the head clamps looked like instruments of torture!) from behind to keep her from moving and becoming a blur.

She met Diana's gaze over Lil's head and rolled her eyes. Their tea was cold, and Diana must be as tired as

Pauline was of waiting for the answer they both saw coming.

"So?" Diana bent to Lillian in her chair. "Should we go? It's almost four o'clock. It's OK if you don't want to," she added kindly, reaching to mimic Pauline's dainty back rub. "It's OK if it's too much."

"Yes, let's," Lillian said bravely, and blew her nose into her handkerchief. "There's no point canceling now. Mr. Mumler is greatly occupied. We're fortunate to have an appointment."

"You mean Gemma, Sue, and Dora are fortunate to have an appointment," Diana corrected. On Cliff's recommendation, they had made their appointment under false pretenses. Lil couldn't help but smile at their daring.

Lil was really much, much prettier, Pauline thought, when she smiled.

Mr. Mumler was detained when they arrived with Cliff as chaperone. The assistant sat them down and brought a tray with tea to occupy them. He asked to interview them separately ("Together, if you please," Cliff insisted, smoothing his little goatee; "I have charge of the reputations of these young ladies").

The assistant nodded, asking them each delicate questions in hushed, reverent tones — about their loved ones and who, on the other side, they would like to hear from — and scribbling notes.

"Hear from?" Lil echoed, alarmed.

"You *do* understand the process?" the young man said, looking up as if Lil were wasting his time. "The human eye can't see them, the spirits, but the camera can."

"We do," Cliff replied. "Thank you."

When the long tale of woe that was Jeremiah wound down, Diana "chose" her dear great-aunt, and then it was Pauline's turn. The assistant readied his fountain pen, but all she could think to say without sarcasm was "Surprise me."

The photographer emerged from his dark closet at last, with bruised circles under his eyes.

His face might have been a merry one, Pauline thought, under other circumstances, but his fate weighed heavily. Anyone could see that. She went third again, and while the photographer disappeared under his dark cloth, poked his head out to reposition the wooden camera, and lifted and replaced the lens cap, Pauline stood as still as she could manage, deciding that Mr. Mumler was almost handsome in a tragic, avuncular way. She began to regret her father's role in his coming demise.

When the day's romantic hero delivered their photographic plates, Lil gasped to see Jeremiah—or a hazy version of him in a Union coat—standing behind her.

Overcome, she buried her face in Pauline's shoulder a moment.

Diana clapped with delight to find her portly Dutch aunt in profile, holding a snapped tulip.

Pauline could only stare at the blur in the chair beside her — bright and reversed on the glass negative.

"Surprise," said Mr. Mumler, bowing in her direction as he walked the tray of negatives back into his dark closet.

Pauline wasn't sure whether to be offended or delighted.

While the photographer developed their cabinet cards, the dour assistant brought Cliff to the desk to square up.

Lil wept, and Pauline and Diana rubbed her back.

In the morning, Diana sent over a servant with a sealed envelope. *See the Herald,* she had written on the calling card inside.

Pauline sent their girl Anna out for both last evening's and this morning's editions: "Spiritualism in Court," read the headlines, and "A Stupendous Fraud," and "The Alleged Spirit Photograph Swindle."

"The intensity of the interest manifested by the public in this case . . ." wrote the *New-York Tribune,* and Pauline felt a wave of sickness. What had seemed a game only yesterday now felt ripe for scandal. Would the police come for her? Would Daddy learn what she had done? Would *she* be called to testify? And if so, what would she say about the thing floating beside her on the cabinet card Mr. Mumler had sent her home with, her own "alleged spirit"?

Surprise.

Pauline closed the paper and hurried up to the room she took over when she stayed at Daddy's Fifth Avenue brownstone in Manhattan. She found the photograph in a pile of yesterday's correspondence but would not look at it. She clapped the cardboard against her chest and tried to decide where best to hide the evidence. She couldn't dispose of the photograph — it had cost too much, for one thing, and it had a certain novelty about it — but Daddy mustn't know. He would never forgive her for undermining his credibility.

Pauline carried the cabinet card into the library, a smaller version of the library at their home in Bridgeport, though most of the books in this collection were for show. Daddy preferred his office, so the library was rarely used, its books rarely opened.

Tugging first at her corset, Pauline looked up and felt a little shiver; she rolled the ladder as far from the dusty Italian puppet theater in the top-right corner as she could get. The toy had been on that high shelf, or the corresponding high shelves at Iranistan and Lindencroft, their country homes, for as long as she could remember.

In her youth, the toy had held a special draw.

Pauline had even tried to climb up and seize it once, after Helen snatched it away and stowed it on the shelf, only to fall off the ladder and twist her ankle. Pauline was babied for a week and banned from ladders (and the library, which was fine; books bored her).

As an additional measure, Mother had Daddy remove the temptation to the mansion in Manhattan. She might have never thought of the puppet theater again if not for Mr. Mumler's photograph.

These days, Pauline was the only one in the family besides Daddy who spent time in their city residence. Her father saw Manhattan as a refuge (from Mother, it was understood), and Caroline and Helen and their families had lives and friends in Connecticut. Pauline had to beg to spend a few weeks in New York with her circle while her husband, Nathan, was away on business. But what she wanted, she usually got.

Feeling a sympathetic pain in her foot just thinking about her mishap in the other library, Pauline climbed only one rung on the ladder.

She slid out a dusty tome with a dull title — *Buffon's Natural History: Quadrupeds, Birds, Fishes* — and tucked her ghostly cabinet card inside. She returned the volume, then stepped down and moved the ladder back to its corner before Daddy could find her out.

On April 21, there was a preliminary hearing into Mr. Mumler's case. The judge would weigh counsel, consider the evidence, and assign the case to a grand jury if appropriate. The trial was in the papers every day, and when it became clear that her own role in the affair was negligible, Pauline began to relax and follow it with interest. Diana, Lil, and Cliff—their entire circle, really, since everyone knew about their outing but had vowed secrecy—followed it, too, holding confabs to discuss the adventure in lurid whispers.

The news accounts tracked Mr. Mumler's rise in New York after fleeing scandal in Boston late last year. By early this year, he'd rebuilt his reputation in New York as the preeminent master of spirit photography. He'd taken portraits of more than five hundred people and was able to purchase a studio at 630 Broadway.

On March 16, a gentleman calling himself William Bowditch came in to commission a portrait with "extras," which was, as far as Pauline could tell, another way of saying dead people. Bowditch, as it happened, was Joseph Tooker, New York City marshal, heading an undercover police sting. Tooker's officers arrested Mr. Mumler on April 12 for "swindling credulous persons" and jailed him in the Tombs.

At the trial, the prosecutor listed nine ways spirit photographs might be faked, though no one seemed sure what the accused's exact methods were. One well-known photographer saw no fraud in Mr. Mumler's technique. Other experts backed the prosecution:

ghostly effects were easy, they said. One chemist boasted that he could photograph "a man with an angel over his head, or with a pair of horns on his head, just as I wish."

And then it was Daddy's turn. He had blasted spirit photography in his book, and now, during cross-examination, Mr. Mumler's lawyer challenged him for the same reasons Pauline had. Why was the accused on trial when Mr. Barnum wasn't? Didn't the show-man make money exploiting a gullible public? Hadn't his museum displayed a dried "mermaid"? "Have you never . . . taken money for the exhibition of spurious curiosities?" the lawyer asked.

Daddy made all the usual arguments and told the crowd about a recent trip to the studio of Abraham Bogardus. He had asked the acclaimed photographer for a spirit image with no humbug about it.

At first, Daddy saw nothing on the glass, he said, other than his own likeness, but when Bogardus made the printed card, he found himself in the shadow of Abraham Lincoln.

Pauline shuddered when she read this—as she imagined many people in the courtroom had done; most everyone remembered exactly where they were and what they were doing when they learned that the pres-ident had been shot in his box at the theater—it was hard to believe four years had passed.

"Persons of all classes, professions, and shades of

opinion were present" in that courtroom, the *New York World* reported. The crowd was one of "the most intelligent that ever assembled in a New York police court," and every one of them wondering, was it a "fraud" or a "miracle"? Did it matter, in the end? And why did Daddy get to have all the fun?

When he came home the night of his testimony, Pauline had already read the evening editions. She followed him into the library while he took off his jacket, begging to see the picture with Mr. Lincoln.

He waved her off, laughing. "It's back at the courtroom. Evidence." His eyes glittered with the old joy. He was happiest when notorious. "But *oh*, I killed them dead, Sweet P.!"

"I know!" she said as he caught her in his big bearish embrace. "The newsboys were shouting it on the street."

She saw over his shoulder that the dusty toy theater had fallen down. It lay crumpled on the carpet beside a few splayed books. But she hadn't gone anywhere near it! Pauline had made a point of staying as far away from it as possible.

Luckily, Daddy was already out the door in search of supper. "Let's go find some celebratory pudding," he called as Pauline lifted her skirts and got down on hands and knees. There were fuzzy little hand-painted puppets everywhere, as if someone had hurled them in a fit. They'd tipped out of the little drawer beneath the theater's stage and rolled under Daddy's desk. Pauline studied each as she collected them, but the toys were so faded it was hard to make them out, apart from a dancing bear and a grinning cat.

In an oddly coherent flash of memory, Pauline remembered her own dollhouse fondly — lost in the blaze at Iranistan. For the first time, she wondered how the theater could have survived the fire at Iranistan when her dollhouse didn't.

She shut the puppets in their compartment, adjusted the tiny velvet curtain, and looked up the ladder. Something told her not to climb it, even though the empty space on the shelf gaped. She had already forgotten her photograph, and which book she had stashed it in. It no longer mattered. The trial would be over soon, and Mr. Mumler was no longer fashionable.

With nowhere to conceal the evidence, Pauline walked the puppet theater to the dumbwaiter and dropped it down. It made a soft *whoosh*.

She would see to it later.

ALL ELEPHANTS
ARE TRAGIC

When entertaining the public, it is best
to have an elephant.

      —P. T. Barnum

Nancy sat up alone in a strange (too-soft) bed at Wavewood, her stepdaughter's cottage on their Bridgeport property, aware that she had slept fitfully and too late. She massaged her lower back, listening into the stillness. The windows were open, and she heard the sloshing of Long Island Sound below — the water had rocked and tossed all night, as she had — but no sounds of workmen yet. No dynamite, if there would be dynamite.

She would hate to miss a minute.

Had Taylor come to bed last night? Nancy hadn't felt his lumbering presence or the tickle of his nightcap against her cheek.

She'd left their family gathering early, as usual. There was a moon, almost full, so she hadn't bothered to light the lamps in the guest room. Nancy had rocked in the wicker chair, reminding herself, as she often did, that the sound spilled into the ocean, that one day a boat would sail her home to England on that ocean. But for now, it was enough to remember that the world was wide.

She had sat and rocked a while, watching the rotating beam of the lighthouse, but then shut her eyes and imagined her house, Marina, alone on the adjacent hill. By tonight it would be — utterly and perfectly alone. Nancy had fallen asleep to the murmur of water, to voices and laughter beyond the guest room wall.

It was long past morning. She slipped from bed and padded to the bay window, peering over at the main property. She was surprised to spot Taylor on Caroline's arm, ambling up the gravel path to the houses. Her stepdaughter was carrying a picnic basket.

Nancy dressed hurriedly, the blood thumping in her ears. This was *her* day.

Caroline's husband, David, looked up over his news sheet when she entered the dining room. Nancy could hear the maid finishing the breakfast dishes in the pantry.

"They've gone out?" she asked, keeping the sting of bewilderment from her voice.

David lifted his glasses and glanced in her general direction. "Yes. You were asleep. Our brood arrived after you turned in last night. Fran's taken the children down to the rocks."

The little cottage would soon swarm with visiting children, grandchildren, and great-grandchildren. They came and went in packs all summer.

She and Taylor were crowded in with the hordes for safety reasons. Nancy had waited patiently, and today, at last, they would tear the old house to the ground. They would raze Waldemere, and Nancy would watch.

After fifteen years of marriage, she couldn't exactly think of herself as "the new" anymore, but her house was new. Marina was his gift to her, and she was Taylor's last hurrah, his last stab at the youthful life he cherished.

But Taylor was also, regrettably, a family man. ("He is *now*," Caroline had teased last night, ribbing him, as she did.)

Taylor's girl Pauline had died young — six years before his circus favorite, Tom Thumb — with measles, but her children and some of Helen's (Helen might just as well be dead, in her father's eyes) would arrive for the season today.

Nancy hoped very much to be sleeping in her own bed tonight.

"And my husband?"

"Your husband," David said, damping his thumb to turn a page, "has gone with my wife to oversee the demolition." He looked up with false solicitude. "Would you care for coffee, Nancy? Jean will be happy to brew some fresh before she goes."

Nancy ignored the question, which was just another way of saying she was a bother. "They've gone out . . . with *a picnic?*"

Now David would know that her previous questions had only been *cloaked* in innocence, that she had seen Taylor and Caroline winding down the path with the basket, but Nancy didn't care. Delicacy and civility got her nowhere in this family.

She could no longer be expected to measure every sting or slight that slipped from her mouth — they didn't — and she knew just what they were up to, amassing at the cottage *now*.

It all began with the salty bouillabaisse last night at dinner. It was Taylor's favorite dish (when well prepared, and would Caroline hear of borrowing their cook?), and his daughter had "raided a local fisherman's stash" and cooked up a pot to "comfort" him in advance.

As if Taylor needed comforting. As if he wasn't as eager to break with the past as Nancy was. It should have been her picnic.

"It's a fine morning," David said with a shrug, "in spite of the day's agenda. Enjoy it." He loaded the words with spite — parroting, as ever.

Oh, I will, Nancy thought. *Every minute.*

She went to fetch her bonnet and parasol.

"Instructions are to keep at least five hundred feet away from the site at all times," David called after when she stepped out into the glare, "for safety's sake!"

Which would put me over the cliff, she thought bitterly, shading her eyes. *And wouldn't that please you lot? One less heir to worry about.*

Taylor was still tottering up the steep hill on Caroline's arm when Nancy reached the gravel. She slowed her step, stopping by the wall to pick out Fran and the children down below on the beach, past the rocks.

The boys were slapping seaweed at each other while their mother leaped out of the way. They were a spirited clan. Nancy gave them that. They could afford to be. She'd had no such luxury as a child. She and her sister had no childhood at all, it sometimes seemed, though they must have done. Nancy remembered little of life before Mum died, and after — Da saw no need to keep the servants — his girls ran the home while he saw to business.

It was through John Fish that Nancy met her husband in the first place. Da had heard Taylor lecture in Manchester, and afterward, he'd told the showman he owed his material success to *The Life of P. T. Barnum*. Da had used the autobiography as a blueprint. When he built his new mill, Nancy had christened it Barnum.

The men became fast friends, and when Da joined Taylor on a trip to Cuba, he let Taylor read Nancy's letters. They so charmed him that he began writing to her himself. "I fell in love with you before I ever saw you," Taylor later admitted.

When he was next in Europe, after Charity's diagnosis, he stopped in at their home in Southport, inviting Nancy and her father to the World's Fair in Vienna. Those ten days were among the happiest of her life, and her fun-loving suitor (he was her suitor, even then — why pretend otherwise?) won her over despite his age, smoothing the way for Da's practical agenda.

Taylor was meeting with an agent in Hamburg when the news reached him, and even with Charity's body waiting in state, he did not go home. He came to Nancy. He came for solace. He came for the silver lining.

They married in secret, on Valentine's Day.

Taylor sailed back to America alone, summoning her in September. Ten days after she docked—ten months after Charity Barnum's death—they married *again*, at the Church of the Divine Paternity on Fifth Avenue.

No one knew the truth. No one ever would.

Taylor and Caroline had exited the path and were no longer visible. All Nancy could see were Waldemere and Marina, side by side on the hill, each imposing in its way.

She panicked, hurrying after. What if the architect and foreman, who had erected the new house just three feet from the old, had their calculations wrong? What if the wrong building collapsed in a heap?

Waldemere was an exalted gingerbread house, a drafty show horse with no electric lights and lousy plumbing. It was dusty and had been full of the wrong sort of bric-a-brac (now packed away along with half of Taylor's Waldemere library and all of the one from New York ... whatever she could subtract without protest). It was a grand house, yes, and full of guest rooms, and those were often full of people, important or otherwise, who required comfort and hospitality at the expense of her time.

Whenever Nancy tried to relax with a breeze on that high bluff with its view of the sound, or sit and read under the great honeysuckle vines, someone showed up with a trunk. Even with capable servants, Waldemere was huge and exhausting. More to it, Nancy felt ill at ease in the family home of a family that would not have her.

She sometimes imagined she saw Charity Barnum on the porch swing with a baby in her lap (Taylor's family was full of babies . . . girls mostly, to his increasing despair), wearing that old-fashioned bonnet from her portrait in the alcove. Nancy could almost hear the monstrous baby wailing, but it would just be seagulls wheeling over the great lawn.

But it wasn't ghosts that plagued Nancy in her Bridgeport solitude.

At first, she had made a point of staying abreast of her husband's work. She would be more than a domestic partner; she would be a trusted friend and adviser. That was the idea of partnership she went in with, but then she got an eyeful of Jim Bailey, that most competent of men, wringing his hands and furiously chewing rubber bands.

Nancy took a step back, and another. Taylor sold the Manhattan property and stopped asking her along on trips. He worked in hotels in New York, Chicago, or wherever his business interests carried him, leaving her behind with her "books and meditations."

Nancy didn't believe in ghosts, but she had traveled

enough with her husband before to place him in time and space, far from her sphere of influence on any given day.

Her thoughts found him riding round a hippodrome track like Nero in a chariot (as he had when the circus last toured England), flirting with a dark-eyed girl about to be fired from a cannon, or shouting down from his box seat for the trainer to open the hippo's cavernous mouth. Taylor was happiest making money, but how these boyish things, the fruits of his labor, made him smile.

When she was a child, Nancy had felt powerless, wanting nothing more than to become an adult and seize control. Taylor wanted to *stay* a child — and to run the show anyway. She had married a mad American child with the money and power to duplicate in the world the constant spectacle shining inside his skull. He might be trapped in the body of an old man now, but he had an empire of childhood to show for it.

As for Nancy, she had the life she had asked and fought for, a gracious life in the country — and the city, when required — access to stimulating people, time to think, read, and write.

She wasn't haunted by ghosts but by tents strung with colored lights, which sprouted like mushrooms on her manicured lawns. There were giants and dwarfs in the hedges, hot-air balloons drifting overhead, wax-works in the conservatory, the flash of spangles in every shadow. Open the garden shed and behold—

The Weird Hairy Family of Burma!
"TOUCH THEM FOR LUCK!"

Nancy had told her doctor during their last session that she couldn't even close her eyes to make it all go away. When she tried, the pandemonium was magnified, as if Taylor's press agent had set up shop in her head and was writing the copy of her life.

SINGULAR PHENOMENON—A TORTOISESHELL CAT NURSING A FAMILY OF SQUIRRELS!

Words and nuance had always been Nancy's currency and solace, but her marriage made a mockery of words.

As she came up over the rise, she saw Taylor and Caroline relaxing in deep deck chairs near the wall overlooking the sound. They had covered a lot of ground, settling as far from the two houses as the layout of the grounds allowed. They were also deep in conversation.

Nancy now spied movement between the houses. Wagons full of men and equipment were arriving, and what seemed like dozens of workers quickly circled the doomed Waldemere with rope and picks and sledgehammers.

She heard the foreman bark instructions as other men unharnessed the horses and removed them to the stables for safety. Taylor waved, and the foreman and architect strode over to him.

Caroline rose and stepped away to leave the men to their business, so Nancy slowed her pace again. She ambled along, dragging her fingers along the hedges. Taylor leaned forward, but he didn't rise from his chair to greet the men. He looked tired and slumped, she thought, though not like last year, when Nancy had actually dared to imagine an end to the odd tragicomedy of her married life.

When an intestinal obstruction left Taylor unable to keep food down, he had taken to his bed, shedding seventy pounds in six months. He became — overnight it seemed, both to him and his startled (young) bride — old. Even when he was up and tottering, he remained frail. "I don't worry about business and never shall again," he told his secretary and agents, anyone who would listen. "Keep me from thinking and working if you can."

They had all heard it before, but Nancy half believed him this time. He really might retire, but it was a little late, wasn't it? To want to come home when he'd stayed away when Nancy — and if she were charitable, Charity before her — needed him most? He might even die, a subject about which, in her heart of hearts, Nancy had mixed feelings. Old though Taylor was, forty years older, exasperating and at times dispiriting though he was, they had begun their life together in utter secrecy under the most romantic of pretenses, and her feelings were complicated.

The invalid had lurked underfoot for most of the year, wringing his hands and making amends with all and sundry, promising himself and Nancy peace and quiet, until one day lightning struck.

How could he go around calling his latest circus enterprise with Jim Bailey the "Greatest Show on Earth" when it *didn't*, in fact, have the biggest, smallest, hairiest . . . and best of everything? P. T. Barnum was one wonder short, and it was time he made England an offer they couldn't refuse.

The elephant brought him back from the brink.

At six and a half tons, eleven and a half feet tall, Jumbo was the largest animal in captivity at the time, a beloved icon at the London Zoo. Taylor had eyed him for some time but never imagined Nancy's countrymen would part with him. It just happened that Jumbo was beginning to throw temper tantrums, dangerous ones, so the zoological society accepted Taylor's offer of ten thousand dollars with relief.

The circus showman was born again.

Sixteen circus horses had pulled while several elephants pushed to deliver the "Monster Elephant" (*"THE TOWERING MONARCH OF HIS MIGHTY RACE, WHOSE LIKE THE WORLD WILL NEVER SEE AGAIN!"*) up Broadway from the Battery in his giant rolling cart.

With help from his British keeper, Scotty, with whom he shared a bottle of beer each night after a hard day's circus work, Jumbo warmed to his new home in Madison Square Garden. Gingerbread replaced English buns as his favorite food.

"Beer can't be good for an elephant," Nancy had objected.

"Beer isn't good for anyone," Taylor said. Many years before Nancy's time, when he was touring Europe with Tom Thumb, he had almost ruined his family and his life under the influence and had sworn off liquor ever since. Back when he was mayor of Bridgeport, he had tried to make everyone else swear off it, too, with mixed results.

In less than four short seasons, Jumbo became Taylor's pride and joy, the star in a crown of wonderful creatures he'd collected over a long career.

The Greatest Show on Earth was performing in St. Thomas, Ontario, that September when disaster struck. Men were loading the menagerie onto trains, with Jumbo and the baby clown elephant, Tom Thumb, meandering toward their "Palace Car," when an unscheduled freight barreled toward them.

As Taylor later told it, putting "drapery" on the story for promotion's sake, Jumbo wheeled around, gathered Tom Thumb close with his long trunk, and flung his costar twenty yards away. He broke the calf's hind leg but saved his life. His sacrifice complete, the noble giant took the locomotive head-on with a mighty trumpeting.

When his beloved and distraught trainer ran to Jumbo's side, the elephant curled Scotty in his trunk and, as one eyewitness put it, "drew him down where that majestic head lay bloodstained in the cinders. Scotty cried like a baby."

Taylor was sad, too, to be sure, at least she had thought so, but here's where things got complicated for Nancy.

When the circus opened the following season, it had a grim new exhibit: the Double Jumbo.

You could come to the circus and see not only Jumbo's skeleton paraded past but his taxidermied skin, followed by a procession of other circus elephants, all dutifully trained to carry big black-bordered hankies to wipe their elephant eyes with. It was a funeral all season long.

It was no way to treat a friend.

As another of her husband's British "acquisitions," Nancy identified with Jumbo. How proud Taylor had been to have a young English "girl" (his endearment: or "my little wife" or "my old woman") on his arm as they traipsed in and out of the best hotels and opera houses after they married, or went sailing with the Strattons and other wealthy friends, so *many* wealthy friends, on their yachts.

Somehow Jumbo's unceremonious end made her

heart ache. It seemed unfair, for one who had lived up to his billing in every way.

A year after the loss of Jumbo, the circus's winter quarters in Bridgeport, the biggest animal training ground in the world, was leveled by fire, killing most of the animals. All Nancy remembered of that night was that poor Gracie the elephant had tried to swim to safety . . . making it all the way to the lighthouse before she sank under the waves. All elephants were tragic, it seemed to Nancy, captives stolen from their homes and made to perform against their wild natures.

Taylor called the winter quarters his "fifth great fire." Fire had savaged her husband's career so regularly that, in jest and if they dared, people called him "Barnum the arsonist."

But about the winter quarters tragedy, too, Taylor was unperturbed.

You fall down. You get up. God has a plan, and it's not our business to understand; we must accept it. He spoke of fate and providence but never sorrow, never regret.

It occurred to Nancy that she had played a decisive role in his swift acceptance of his first wife's death, and that her husband might, given the chance, recover with like haste if she herself died.

She would be lucky if he didn't stuff her and mount her in one of his sideshows (*"A PRODIGIOUS SIGHT!"*).

Jumbo's unceremonious end had rattled Nancy

to her core not because she had loved the animal, but because Taylor had.

His voice now rose over the hammering and pounding by the house, calling out a farewell to his architect and foreman, who walked back to the work site. Caroline remained aloof by the wall, her hands flat on stone. Her posture was defeated, and Nancy wished she could acknowledge her sadness, woman to woman, but they all had their roles to play. Caroline was the loyal one who would take a sword for her father, be his general. Pauline, in her day, was the grateful clown, always pretty and bright and game for a laugh. Helen was the prodigal, the baffling one who couldn't keep to script.

As for Nancy, she was a former stage actor with wit and sparkle, happy to mask herself. Taylor had hired her to act the role of accomplished and conversational young wife, a proper English girl from the country to play minx in private, and Nancy could flip on a dime, though she couldn't always get the timing right. Taylor set out to direct her and succeeded.

From the first, Nancy had overestimated herself. She sent photographs back home to show her sister and friends how gracious it was, how exciting, her life in America, and how settled her heart and mind. But it was a lie. She grew more isolated by the year.

Everyone in the family was doomed to act out their

prejudices, to play as cast. He never had to pit them against one another. He had only to combine them, as he'd combined Commodore Nutt and the giantess Anna Swan. It wasn't just novelty Taylor understood but chemistry, how certain combinations led to certain outcomes, and the only acceptable outcome was his sovereignty.

Caroline had returned to her seat at his side, and Nancy resumed her stroll, sticking close to the hedge walk to appear occupied. She picked wildflowers from the edge — landscaping had gone to the devil since construction began — twirling a buttercup under her chin and watching the workers, or their work, with interest.

Nancy breathed in and began to cross the great lawn. She imagined them — Caroline, at least — frowning as she approached and kept her eyes downcast, holding up her hem and glancing at Marina from time to time for confidence. It was an elegant house under Nancy's influence: Queen Anne–style brick and stone with English ivies and piazzas. She and Taylor had divided their time between New York and Waldemere for years before she felt comfortable enough to ask for a home of her own; once he consented, Nancy haggled with him over every detail. It would be *her* house, after all, when he died, and supposedly that was the point, to build an efficient, modern home that Nancy could manage alone.

Waldemere. When they came back from their honeymoon in Saratoga, her new "family" had greeted them on the porch in high-mourning clothes. Though Charity had been dead ten months, they had hung a fresh wreath on the door. That was the first time in her entire life that Nancy Fish retired early with a headache. She had once believed her nerves were as hard and flawless as the right diamond. She had mocked women like her predecessor, Charity Barnum, with their ailments and rest cures.

How ambitious she had been ... once.

She was Nancy Fish Barnum now and had spent three months out of the last year at a sanatorium under the care of Dr. Anton Politzer.

Taylor had tried to console her the next morning by laughing the porch incident off—the black crepe, the sickly lilies. "Weddings, funerals," he said. "Any excuse for a new dress."

"My children," Nancy told people in those early days, including reporters intrigued by the world-famous showman and his young trophy wife, with a strained smile, "are disrespectful. *Most* disrespectful. For they call me Nancy. My grandchildren call me Aunt Nancy." Nancy was younger than all of her stepdaughters, even Pauline, and they never forgave her for it. To this day—apart from Barnie, Helen's eldest—only the great-grandchildren, three times removed, accepted her and called her Grandma: no prize, really.

A great hammering racket started up as she arrived. Nancy kissed Taylor on the cheek. He took her hand mechanically and seemed cheerful enough, though Caroline was buttering bread with tremendous force of purpose, her brow furrowed.

"We're making sandwiches." He kissed the back of Nancy's hand. "She has plums, too, don't you, Caro?"

Nancy looked at her stepdaughter and knew better than to accept. "Oh, no, thank you. I've had breakfast," she lied.

There was no third chair for her, so Nancy hovered awkwardly by her husband's and at length perched on its arm. Caroline ought to have known better than to let him recline all the way back in such a deep chair. It would take a harem to haul him out again, and the aches and pains would stay all night.

The rhythmic battering of picks and sledge-hammers caught them up and held them in thrall. The air filled with dust; a great column of it rose up and wafted. Luckily, what breeze there was came off the water and away from the onlookers, but Nancy supposed it would coat Marina, sticky as cremated bone.

They would disassemble Waldemere stone by stone, it seemed, and cart it off that way. Not all of the horses had been led to shelter, Nancy now saw. Two big Belgians stood attached to a long wagon on the safe side of Marina, waiting to haul away debris.

They sat there all day, and for once she was not

restless in one of his audiences. It was more gripping than the opera.

Jenny Lind had nothing on demolition.

Taylor finished one bread-and-butter sandwich and requested another. Nancy stood up and stretched. She brought back a buttercup and held it under his chin. "You like butter," she announced over the noise.

"What?"

"You *like butter!*"

He glanced from his half-eaten sandwich to her flower and smiled with all his dentures.

If Nancy were a cat, she would have been purring under the racket.

More men would come to fill Waldemere's cellar hole and cover it with grass sod. Landscapers would plant shrubs and trees.

You would never know the old house had been there.

Nancy tried not to look at Caroline, not to note the way her "mature" stepdaughter had to keep sneaking a knuckle past either cheek to erase tears.

It may have been compassion, or just discretion, but Nancy wondered as she sometimes did: Would all of their lives have been different — better — if Taylor's daughters had found it in their hearts to treat her like family? If they had forgiven her youth and ambition — and Nancy had forgiven them their history?

"I wish Helen was here."

Caroline had just blurted it out, as if in answer — a petulant child's answer. Nancy smiled politely into the distance. *(THE CAROLINA TWINS! Although insepara-bly joined, yet their individual movements are easy and grace-ful. They are lively and vivacious, and are pronounced by all who have seen them as the GREATEST CURIOSITY in the WORLD!)*

"Papa? Don't you wish? She should be here."

Taylor had never looked more doddering to Nancy or more dear.

"It was Iranistan she loved," he said flatly.

If he meant to console Caroline, he had failed.

Overcome, she excused herself and skulked back to the cottage, leaving the picnic basket behind on the grass.

Nancy had no idea how she would lift her husband out of that chair when the time came. *(A CURI-OUS MORTUARY MEMORIAL TO WASHINGTON AND LINCOLN, Ten Feet High, and composed of over Two Million Sea Shells!)*

But nothing could spoil her mood now. With the furious pounding from the work site as encourage-ment, Nancy couldn't stop smiling.

Her mind buzzed with plans and schemes. Marina had a music room, her sanctuary. Taylor's was the pri-vate first-floor office, his "Growler," he called it because he would growl if he caught you in there. He was becoming secretive about accounts and sensitive about his "heirs." Designed around a large open fireplace and overlooking the gardens, the room was bright with mirrors, signed circus portraits, and framed news clippings.

There was a storage room attached to the office with stacks of dusty crates inside. The presence of these crates, sentimental hoardings from both New York and Waldemere, had worried Nancy no end. She now resolved to sort through and distribute "the old house" as appropriate to the family, with or without Taylor's consent. *(GEOLOGICAL, CONCHOLOGICAL, MUMISMATIC COLLECTIONS, SPECIMENS OF NATURAL HISTORY, PAINTINGS, HISTORICAL RELICS, ETC.!)*

She paced a moment, then walked behind his chair and rested her hands on her husband's shoulders, kneading lightly, though it was balance she wanted, not intimacy.

Nancy felt a sick, sweet shudder when the last of the facade fell.

The workmen whooped and cheered, brushing chalky dust from their hands and clothes, and she realized that she had been holding her breath, perhaps ever since she stepped off that steamer in New York Harbor. All the years of trying to win people over, earn her keep, keep her head and heart about her, had worn her down. Now, at last, she felt she could breathe. This was the last word.

They sat out there until Waldemere was gone, every stone — until dozens of dusty, strong-armed men were swinging birch brooms in a surreal dance, and the sun spread like honey on the grass, and the shadows leaned.

It was only when the mosquitoes began to bite that Nancy realized why Taylor was so quiet.

He wasn't choked with emotion—grief *or* joy. He was simply an old man who had dozed off in his chair. She looked up at Marina, dark on the hill.

Luckily, they didn't have far to walk.

WHAT MAKES YOU THINK
WE WANT YOU HERE?

I have seldom mentioned my wife and children . . .
yet they have always been dearer to me than all
things . . . No place on earth has ever been so
attractive to me as my home.

— P. T. Barnum

G randpop was dead, and Barnie was nervous.

She didn't much remember being a little child, but as a youth she was so shy and nervous she sometimes found it hard to hear people, hard to understand what they were saying, what they wanted from her. Life had seemed a mist, a haze, a *cloud* of nervous. Barnie coasted through it with her head down.

When she was thirteen, the same year her mother left, a doctor told Dad she was hard of hearing.

It wasn't so — Barnie heard fine — but it was convenient. For most of that summer, she listened only when she liked.

The entire extended family had been at Waldemere for a clambake, weighing the pros and cons of sending Barnie to a special school for the deaf, when Aunt Caroline stuck a pin in. She sneaked over while Barnie had her back to the others. She clapped so loudly beside Barnie's left ear that her niece wheeled and leaped nearly out of her skin.

"Just as I thought." Aunt Caroline chuckled at Barnie's hangdog expression. "She's exactly like her mother at that age."

Barnie's face burned, but no one berated her. No one seemed angry or even surprised. She gave them a sheepish smile, and her sympathetic tribe smiled back, even Grandpop (who more typically frowned at any mention of Helen Buchtel). Aunt Caroline had nailed it, said their faces.

Barnie did the best she could, but there was no denying that her family was, to her, a different species, as tigers were from turtles, and she felt destined to disappoint them and be disappointed in turn. The one person she understood had abandoned them to move to Colorado with her doctor husband, and things hadn't made sense since.

That person was her mother, who wrote Barnie and her sisters (separately) a letter from Denver every week for the rest of their lives. "Helen Maria Barnum Hurd Buchtel" said the careful script in the envelopes' return address box, but as far as she and her father and sisters — and Grandpop, more than anyone — were concerned, only "Helen Buchtel" counted.

Barnie never answered the letters. She collected them in her favorite hatbox. The paper coating on the hatbox showed an exotic jungle scene. She didn't know if her sisters opened or answered the letters. Helen Buchtel was an embarrassing subject and, in time, a forbidden one.

Barnie hadn't been invited into the sickroom to stand by Grandpop's deathbed at the end. Like her cousin Jessie (and others in the grand and "double-grand" category), Barnie had paid last call the night before, with

Frank and their children, though Grandpop was uncon-
scious when they came in. He had drooled, and Jessie
wiped his lips on her lace sleeve, then poked delicately
at his knuckles to see whether he was warm.

But along with Aunts Nancy and Caroline, the pastor, the doctors, and Grandpop's trusty valet, Helen
Buchtel *was* admitted into the great showman's death
chamber. She was his daughter, after all, who arrived
alone all the way from Denver on the morning train,
"under the wire," as Aunt Nancy put it.

Hidden behind a curtain, Barnie had watched
Helen Buchtel arrive (petite and weathered bronze in
that western way, a touch gray around the edges but
with a familiar spark in her hazel eyes) and shake hands
with Nancy in the entryway to Marina. It was the first
time the two women had ever met, though Grandpop
and Aunt Nancy had been married a long time.

It was also the first time Barnie had laid eyes on
her mother in all these years. She was thirty-one but
felt exactly as she had at age thirteen, during the "scandal" of her mother's affair and divorce. Out of sight, out
of mind.

She'd been dodging Helen Buchtel, leaving every
room her mother entered. It was no easy feat—her
mother kept reaching for Barnie with her eyes—but
wherever P. T. Barnum's prodigal daughter went, the
curious monopolized her attentions. Barnie was good
at avoiding people. But she would hate to have to

look away if Helen Buchtel managed to meet her eyes directly.

The family held a private memorial at Marina before the public church service. Small and simple, as Grandpop wanted it. Barnie lurked in back, though Frank and the children tried to wave her forward as discretion allowed. She hardly heard the pastor's words or the circle of recitations by family members and close friends. Barnie was working too hard to contain herself and keep her eyes down.

When it was over, their carriages paraded through Bridgeport behind the coffin.

The day was cold and dismal. The town seemed draped from step to steeple in black crepe and stank of lilies. Flags flew at half-mast, and neighbors and townsfolk had tacked news clippings and grainy likenesses of Grandpop to their barns and shop fronts, just as circus "advance" men tacked up posters. There were wreaths on every door.

It was remarkable, really. Maybe Barnie hadn't known quite how "big" a man he was. Her grandfather may have been mayor once, and an impresario always, but to her he was just Grandpop (that old trickster).

South Church was the only one in town large enough to hold a Barnum-size service, and it was already filled to bursting when they got there. An even more massive crowd was assembled out front, spilling off sidewalks into the street. Some were just there

for the arrival and departure of the funeral cortege—
to say they had been there—but most were genuine.
Barnie could see it in their faces as they parted to let the
family pass.

She walked in beside her husband, Frank, and their
children, half expecting to find trapezes dangling from
the church ceiling and pink ladies soaring overhead.
There *were* circus folk in the crowd, and it was interesting to spot them in their street clothes, like seeing your
childhood schoolmaster at the butcher's.

Barnum and Bailey's would not play Madison
Square Garden that night, Mr. Bailey had decreed. "The
dearly departed wouldn't approve of the pause," he
had told the family when he arrived for the service at
Marina, "but today the show must *not* go on."

It took some time for everyone to quiet down,
even after the pastor took the podium. Dr. Collyer had
long white hair and a surging voice. Every sentence he
uttered prompted waves of murmuring.

Barnie closed her eyes. The strain of locating and
avoiding Helen Buchtel was beginning to wear on her.
She let the pastor's voice rinse away or at least dilute
her worry.

"P. T. Barnum was a born fighter," Dr. Collyer
thundered, "for the weak against the strong, for the
oppressed against the oppressor."

Frank took her hand under her crackling mourning cloak, but Barnie couldn't feel his touch through

the glove and wished she could. At nearly the same moment, the pastor used the word *melancholy*, the same word that had brought Barnie and her husband together. They were strangers on a train that day, in facing seats, and without leaning forward in any untoward way, Frank asked, "Why so melancholy?" It shocked Barnie, that someone she didn't know, a man, would ask such an intriguing personal question.

"I'm not sure," she replied honestly.

They were engaged within the month.

"The good heart, tender as it was brave, would always spring up at the cry for help and rush on with the sword of assistance."

Melancholy was a word that tasted like a plum, Barnie thought. It rolled in her mouth like a ripe plum, and she could never understand how it got confused with sadness. Today she was not sad. Only melancholy. Grandpop died a very old man. He had lived larger than anyone she would ever know, and thousands had come out in the damp today to cheer him off on his final voyage. There was nothing sad about that, though Aunt Caroline's chapped face had been buried in a lace handkerchief for weeks.

Barnie spotted Helen Buchtel in the first row, the back of her erect head. She wanted to look at Frank — he could calm her without a word sometimes, that mild, kind face — but it seemed wrong to turn away from the pulpit.

> *"This was not all that made him loved, for the good cheer of his nature was like a halo about him."*

The next thing Barnie knew, they were singing "Auld Lang Syne," and people were snuffling into handkerchiefs.

Pallbearers carried the lily-covered casket out of the church, and the whole show went the mile to Mountain Grove Cemetery, where Grandpop's remains would join Grandmother Charity's in the simple family plot. Barnie stole a glance at Aunt Nancy when they got there, wondering how it felt to relinquish him that way, so to speak.

Many hundreds of mourners would mill about after the service, shooting the breeze and reminiscing, and Barnie almost wished she could stay with them, but the family pushed on.

After their public duties were complete and all fifty-three pages of Grandpop's (oft-revised) last will and testament had been read, after lawyers had placed his "best piano," his stereoscopic slide collection, his marble bust of Jenny Lind, his silver tea set, his gold Iranistan ring, and what must have been a million dollars sliced up like pie (Barnie herself, Frank and the runts were pleased to hear, would receive a substantial sum), there remained only the "small orders of business," as Aunt Nancy put it.

There were crates at Marina, a great many crates that needed divvying. Nancy wanted to expedite. She wanted her house back.

Barnie was supposed to hate Nancy because everyone else did, but as soon as her youthful "aunt" had arrived in Bridgeport (riding a familiar wave of gossip), Barnie decided to make her a special project. Maybe watching a person fight so hard to enter a family, she reasoned, would help her understand her mother, who had fought so hard to get out of one.

The last days at Marina with Grandpop had been sweet. He loved to watch the gulls wheel outside his window and sent Barnie (repeatedly . . . it became their game) to lay crusts of bread down for them. As long as he could still hold the pages and squint, he read his evening *Tribune*, plus poetry, magazines, and scripture, and when he no longer could, one of the girls read aloud to him.

On one memorable day, the *New York Evening Sun* ran his death notice. Grandpop wasn't dead yet, but it was a favor. P. T. Barnum wanted to read his obituary, and his journalist pals obliged.

He gathered the family together for the occasion, and they propped him up in bed. He beamed while Aunt Nancy read the newspaper's good-bye to "the Great and Only Barnum."

Grandpop had asked that "the Children's Friend" be added to his likeness on certain circus posters and ads, as if his only debt now was to childhood, and in those last days he seemed to see the family through a mysterious new lens. Foggy and anxious all month (*who was missing?*), tender with every child, grandchild, and great-grandchild, he peered into each face intently.

But when he could no longer sit up in bed, telegrams were sent, and Barnie began to panic.

Of course Helen Buchtel would come "home" to Bridgeport.

To keep busy, Barnie helped Aunt Nancy lug crates and boxes to the big table in his office while people drifted in and out of the sickroom. Nancy thanked Barnie for being there, and Barnie felt sorry for her, so alone in their midst.

Today, on Nancy's behalf, Barnie asked Aunt Caroline to rally those who would want to be present. Caroline had the biggest voice and no trouble drawing people in from the porches and the cottage next door.

Barnie claimed a chair at the far end of the table, behind the globe on its Italian hardwood stand, and kept her eyes down as her mother filed in with her aunt and a few stragglers. She felt her face burn as everyone settled expectantly around the table.

Without delay, Aunt Nancy began handing things around: letters the archivist had refused, stacks of museum and circus clippings, photographs, books. The quiet party passed and picked through them. In another family, Barnie thought, on another day, they might have been snapping beans together in the kitchen.

"Before I forget"—Nancy walked away, returning with a folder from the desk—"Jim Bailey left this for you, Helen. He said your father wanted you to have it . . . or that you might want it."

Helen Buchtel opened it to find a cover and yellowed clippings from *Frank Leslie's Illustrated Newspaper*. She spread the pages on the table. Like everyone else and in spite of herself, Barnie tilted her head to read.

"Jack!" Helen Buchtel cried out, lifting a page. She squinted at one of the captions, then looked up at the perplexed majority. Her eyes had a mysterious shine. "I never knew!"

Barnie could only make out the name of the article, "Barnum's Animals: The Victims and the Victors," and that there were engravings alongside, animals in dramatic poses framed by fire or wrecked trains.

Aunt Caroline began circulating paper again, but Helen Buchtel wasn't finished. Mr. Bailey had attached a scrawled note, and she read it aloud absently. "'He's made quite a name for himself and credits you with "discovering" him. Your father took him under his wing.'"

Helen Buchtel was beaming. "This is the bear that survived the second fire." She tapped the picture with her fingernail and kept looking up at them hopefully (didn't they see how *important* this was?).

What she failed to understand, Barnie thought, was that no one knew what in blue blazes she was talking about. Helen Buchtel was the most unknowable person Barnie knew, and there were a million important things *she* had missed. Unknowable things.

Caroline carried on, plucking a cabinet card from a pile. "Where did you find this, Nancy?" She passed the photo to Helen Buchtel, who was forced to close her precious folder and inspect it.

"It's Pauline." Helen Buchtel flipped it over to read the inscription: "'Specialty by Mumler.'"

"Where did it come from?" Aunt Caroline repeated with that edge in her voice that meant she had it in for someone. "We have so few of her."

Barnie had found the photograph, not Nancy, and she knew she had to speak up and spare her "aunt," but for a long moment, the words wouldn't come.

"It fell out of a book," she managed, at last, in a small voice.

Barnie cast down her eyes quickly when her mother smiled over at her. Helen Buchtel set the picture aside as if to turn the subject. "We have very few pictures of *any* of us." She lifted one of the many cabinet cards of General Tom Thumb. "Papa always liked them better."

"Them?" Nancy busied herself emptying the last crate onto the table. Nancy hardly knew Barnie's mother (Barnie hardly knew Barnie's mother), but Helen and Aunt Caroline were very close. Wouldn't a sister of Caroline's be Nancy's enemy by association? Barnie would have assumed the same thing.

"His performers," Helen Buchtel added. "They gave him joy. We never did."

Aunt Caroline grumbled, "Speak for yourself." But just last week, after a turn with Grandpop, she had confided to Barnie in the kitchen, "I always played second fiddle to tiny men and nightingales."

It had seemed strange to Barnie at the time, that her aunt would mourn him before he was even dead, as if her father had been gone for years.

All it took was a glance at the table to see that the "personal" items removed from the old man's office and library were mostly cabinet cards and clippings about snake charmers and lady riders and tattooed men, the people he collected.

Helen Buchtel turned the photograph of Pauline over again, asking, almost nonchalantly, "Where's the spirit?"

Exasperation was Aunt Caroline's native state, and her eyes rolled. "What *spirit*, Helen? What are you talking about?"

"Wasn't Mr. Mumler the man who made photographs with spirits? The one Papa testified against?"

That stumped everyone.

"Pauline must have sat for him before the trial." Helen Buchtel tapped the cabinet card with her index finger. "But she's alone here."

"Why *shouldn't* she be alone? It's a portrait." Aunt Caroline shook her head. "*Honestly*, Helen."

The sisters hadn't missed a beat, Barnie supposed. Her mother and aunt had picked up right where they left off, as if the years and the miles had never parted them.

Helen Buchtel flipped idly through another box. "Well, either way. We aren't *in* any of these photographs. We aren't . . . here."

"I would ask you," braved Aunt Nancy, "to keep these observations to yourself today, Helen. They are subjective, at best, and you've been gone a long time."

As if I had a choice, her expression told them.

Aunt Nancy kneaded her temple. "It isn't your place to criticize."

"Oh, won't you just *hush*, Nancy?" Aunt Caroline startled them all with her vehemence. "You don't know anything. You don't know . . . us."

Nancy held her head as if it balanced a book. "What makes you think you can speak to me that way?" She swiveled to exempt Barnie, one hand raised, and then back to the others. "You are vicious, spoiled creatures. Both of you! I never hurt you. What makes you think —?"

"What makes you think we want you here?"

"*Here* is where I live. And I would beg you to remember it. I am mistress of this house." Nancy waved her arms and breathed in sharply. It *was* her house, at least for now. She had a fifty-three-page document to prove it.

"Jessie shouldn't have to find her mother's picture in a discarded pile," Aunt Caroline entreated them all. "It's the only one I've ever seen of Pauline that young. Jessie might like it . . . presented to her."

She cleared her throat and tried to take Helen Buchtel's hand as if they were still children. Did death turn everyone into children again? Barnie wondered. More than once this week, she had wished Helen Buchtel would gather her up, as her mother would have done once, whether Barnie objected or not. "Let's go, Helen. It seems our company isn't welcome."

To her credit, Helen Buchtel called a halt to it. "Not now, Caro. This isn't the time." She looked straight at Barnie. "I'd like to stay and talk to my daughter."

The room held its breath.

Aunt Caroline crossed to the door with a shrug and a faint smile on her lips. It was her "dream" to see her nieces reunited with their mother. "We'll go through these things later — in *private*, Nancy, if you please. The double-grands might also like some things."

Nancy pretended to tidy a moment. "I'll lie

down," she said, "and rest my eyes awhile . . . if you'll excuse me."

Barnie was left staring fixedly at the cabinet card without a ghost.

She tried to imagine having Aunt Caroline's fearsome confidence—*What makes you think we want you here?*—or Grandpop's, for that matter. Was there ever a time when her boisterous grandfather had felt unwanted? Barnie's dad had worked for his father-in-law and told Barnie once the "secret" of Grandpop's success: "A thing can fail, but he never panics. He figures out how to rotate that thing or move the spotlight and show it at a newly profitable angle."

It was Grandpop who renamed Barnie—on her thirteenth birthday—a few weeks after Helen Buchtel abandoned them and moved west. He claimed it confused him, addressing his granddaughter as her namesake, though he seemed more troubled by it than confused. Her middle name was Barnum, a moniker Grandpop meant to immortalize: in the will he offered cousin Cliff $25,000 to claim it for *his* middle name. But it was no proper address, so Grandpop shortened her nickname to Barnie, and that took.

Even Barnie was pleasantly surprised at how suddenly and effortlessly she became someone else.

"Barnie" grew up, got married, and had two little ones of her own. She quit being nervous, or so nervous, but then Grandpop decided to die — and Helen Buchtel came east by train — and the nervous flooded back. *So how do I do it, Grandpop? Rotate the spotlight,* she thought desperately, *away from* me?

Barnie stared down at the picture of the tiny General with his tiny thumbprint face. It was soothing in a way the photo of Aunt Pauline wasn't.

Helen Buchtel sat in the chair next to her, lifting the card. "It broke my heart to hear he was gone."

Barnie thought she meant Grandpop, at first, but she peeked up and found Helen Buchtel studying the photograph of General Tom Thumb.

"When I was a girl," she said, "I used to think I'd marry Tom. I thought he would grow, or I'd stop growing, and we'd get married."

Helen Buchtel never seemed to stop talking, and Barnie wondered whether she was as nervous as Barnie was. She certainly hoped so.

"He was a very little boy when he came to live with us, but he seemed so old . . . almost wise. And funny and kind." She looked up, remembering. "How he *indulged* Frances."

Barnie had always wondered about the girl who would have grown up to be her aunt. Frances Irena Barnum had died without a trace, it seemed. There were no portraits in the rotunda, no unlabeled cabinet cards or daguerreotypes in Nancy's crates that might've been the youngest Barnum sibling. Barnie had looked.

Today, though, she had noticed the little stone in the family plot with just the one word, *Frances.*

What was she like? She met Helen Buchtel's eyes with great difficulty.

"Her temper scared *everyone,*" she said, "even your grandpop—but boy, Frances loved Tom. Adored him! She was furious when they took him away to tour Europe. She didn't understand where they'd gone or why they left her."

I know the feeling, Barnie thought, and felt Helen Buchtel trying to look in through the window of her eyes, trying to find her, but Barnie closed them. She shut her eyes tight. Her whole body stiffened as Helen Buchtel tried to take her hand. Barnum was a grown woman! She recovered the hand and turned her face to the window. Barnie would not be found.

But she remembered it now, how her mother had magically known, at times, what she needed to hear. She would—or seemed to—answer questions before Barnie asked them. When she left them to live in her precious mountains, that had left, too. Barnie had felt doubly alone, for her sisters offered no comfort and behaved as if they needed none. She was oldest and the weakest, too attached, the one Dad said their mother had "ruined."

"Walk out with me." Helen Buchtel smoothed Barnie's stiff hands—mirrors of her own but younger—on the table as if Barnie's knuckles were wrinkles in a doily. "Do me that much? It's stuffy in here. Let's walk out and take our shoes off." She stood up, brushing down her skirts, and crossed to the window. "The tide's out."

And so it was that two grown women with bare feet, swaddled head to toe in black, walked a mile along a windswept beach on the same day an old showman was placed in a lily-covered casket. The casket was placed in a cedar box. The cedar box was plunged into a deep brick vault and covered with a two-ton slab of stone.

It was a gray April day with light drizzle. Clouds skidded over the sound. The women flowed together and apart, using their shawls as collecting aprons. They traipsed over sandbars, dragging their hems through salt, lifting shells and pretty stones and mermaid's purses. Sometimes Helen Buchtel walked over to look in Barnie's apron and assess her haul, but to Barnie's great relief, neither spoke.

Her hands were numb by the time they started back, and before they mounted the steep staircase to Marina, her mother caught her arm. "Did you read my letters, Helen?"

Barnie.

"No," she said. "I didn't."

Loose from its pins, her mother's hair whipped in the wind. "I hope you will one day. Everything in them is . . . true," she said, but the wind took the word away. She held back her hair with one chapped hand. "Still true. You were taken from me, and I never forgave him for it — my father — until today."

What had simmered in Barnie all morning came to a boil. Stubbornness.

"He never understood," her mother went on. "I didn't leave so I could do as I please...."

All Barnie wanted in the world was to cover her ears, so she dumped her bounty out onto the sand. One delicate bleached seashell snagged on the fabric, and for no reason, Barnie slipped it into her pocket.

"I left so I could be who I please."

Whom. Barnie turned her apron back into a shawl and blew on raw hands, starting up the steep steps to Marina.

At the top, Aunt Caroline was waiting. She'd watched them from here, Barnie supposed, and now, as they emerged, she pulled them close.

Barnie stepped back — thirteen again and embarrassed — but felt the perfect little porcelain ear in her pocket. She rolled the shell in her fingers and listened to the husky murmuring of her mother and aunt, who held each other a long time.

Finally Aunt Caroline stepped back. "All those obituaries!" She shook Helen's shoulders playfully. "And lists! Lists of achievements ... lists of assets ... lists of every one he's 'survived' by ..." Aunt Caroline let her arms sink to her sides and glanced back and forth between them. "Will we, I wonder?"

"Will we what?" asked Helen.

"Survive him?"

Barnie stepped into their circle again, kneading her little shell. She spoke to her cold feet as the older women stroked her hair. "He'd hate us," she said, "if we didn't."

A NOTE ABOUT THE STORIES

You may wonder, *Is this a book of fiction or a book of nonfiction?*

It's fiction, to be sure — historical fiction with a basis in fact.

Is it a novel? Or a collection of stories?

It's a collection of linked stories, meant to resonate together, a bit like chapters in a novel but without the linear arc.

And why the pictures? Are they real?

For me, the world of Barnum is as much a visual narrative as a story in words. The spectacle and artifice of that world are tucked away in archives, like the Library of Congress and the Bridgeport Public Library, in the form of daguerreotypes, cabinet cards, and other forms of early photography, lithographs, etchings, exhibit catalogs, posters, flyers, and handbills. And a moving photograph like Mathew Brady's portrait of young Charles Stratton (page 21) truly speaks a thousand words.

These pictures — and many others — were as much a part of my research as biographies and primary sources, and there's only one "humbug" in the lot: the portrait on page 205 is not of Pauline Barnum and does not contain a spirit.

* * *

The time line and most of the historical events in these tales are more or less accurate, too. Barnum did display a "Fejee Mermaid" and tour General Tom Thumb in Europe, where the tiny man charmed royalty. He did make his young charge a world-class celebrity . . . and a millionaire.

Charles Stratton and Lavinia Warren—the Brad and Angelina of their day—really were married, and they were feted at the White House during the Civil War. Abraham Lincoln's son Robert really did disapprove.

William Mumler ran a trendy studio in Manhattan that claimed to capture sitters alongside the spirits of their dearly departed, and there really was a trial, at which Barnum testified.

Barnum brought Jenny Lind, the Swedish Nightingale, to America (where she was unknown) at enormous expense, making her a celebrity and household name. He "collected"—and often exploited—living curiosities, including the Nova Scotia giantess Anna Swan (who later met and married a fellow giant, by the way, a Kentucky gentleman named Martin Van Buren Bates). Some of the showman's performers suffered acutely; others became wealthy celebrities admired by presidents and queens.

Barnum's family, too, suffered: neglect always, and sometimes cruelty—well documented in the case of his first wife, Charity, who did in fact have a severe panic attack on the steps at Niagara Falls. He left her there.

Barnum lost five of his homes and business ventures to devastating fires in which scores of wild animals he also collected died heartbreaking and horrible deaths.

All but two of the major characters in these stories, the narrators of "Beside Myself" and "The Bearded Lady's Son," existed in fact, including Barnum's four daughters: Caroline, Helen, Frances, and Pauline.

The "humbug" here (Frances's ghost notwithstanding) is the characters' private lives, their inner worlds, which I wholly imagined, based on what I knew about their public lives.

Barnum himself doesn't much figure into the stories. As I see it, "the sun of the amusement world from which all lesser luminaries borrow light"—to quote one of the showman's ads—had more than enough ink, quite a bit of it generated by him and printed in mammoth bold type.

In the end, I was more interested in giving voice to the marginalized women in his life and, inasmuch as possible, to the real and talented entertainers, human and animal, the showman built his entertainment empire on. This book is dedicated to them.

If you're curious to learn more about Barnum's world, read, with a grain of salt, the showman's colorful autobiography, *The Life of P. T. Barnum, Written by Himself*. Candace Fleming's *The Great and Only Barnum: The Tremendous, Stupendous Life of Showman P. T. Barnum* is also a fine place to start, as is the excellent *P. T. Barnum: America's Greatest Showman*, by Philip B. Kunhardt Jr., Philip B. Kunhardt III, and Peter W. Kunhardt.

IMAGE CREDITS

[1/"The Mermaid"]
p. 1
P. T. Barnum's Fejee (also "Feejee," "Fiji") Mermaid
Wikimedia Commons

[2/"The Mysterious Arm"]
p. 21
Charles Stratton ("General Tom Thumb") in traveling clothes, standing on a table, Mathew Brady's studio, 1844–1860
Library of Congress Prints and Photographs Division
(LC-USZ62-109908)

[3/*"Returning a Bloom to Its Bud"*]
p. 51
American Falls from Goat Island, Niagara, New York,
1898–1931.
The Miriam and Ira D. Wallach Division of Art, Prints and Photographs: Photography Collection, The New York Public Library. New York Public Library Digital Collections, http://digitalcollections.nypl.org/items /510d47d9-a1a3-a3d9-e040-e00a18064a99.

[4/"Beside Myself"]
p. 75

Lithograph of opera singer Jenny Lind, 1847
Library of Congress Prints and Photographs Division
(LC-DIG-pga-07285)

[5/"We Will Always Be Sisters"]
p. 107
Lithograph of Iranistan, P. T. Barnum's Bridgeport,
Connecticut, mansion, 1852
Library of Congress Prints and Photographs Division
(LC-DIG-pga-04090)

[6/"The Fairy Wedding"]
p. 129
Charles Stratton ("General Tom Thumb"); his bride,
Lavinia Warren; her sister Minnie; and fellow entertainer
"Commodore" Nutt, in wedding finery, 1863
Library of Congress Prints and Photographs Division
(LC-DIG-ppmsca-52223)

[7/"An Extraordinary Specimen of Magnified
Humanity"]
p. 151
Anna Haining Swan Bates, the Nova Scotia Giantess (date
unknown)
Author's collection

[8/"The Bearded Lady's Son"]
p. 183

Artist's view of the disastrous July 13, 1865, fire at Barnum's
American Museum, with a New York City policeman squaring
off against wild animals escaping the blaze
Frank Leslie's Illustrated News, March 21, 1868
Author's collection

[9/"It's Not Humbug If You Believe It"]
p. 205
A "spirit" photograph (in the style of William Mumler) of a
young woman roughly the same age as Pauline Barnum in this
story (date unknown)
Author's collection

[10/"All Elephants Are Tragic"]
p. 221
Barnum circus poster showing the "Great Jumbo's Skeleton,"
1888
Library of Congress Prints and Photographs Division
(LC-DIG-ppmsca-32620)

[11/"What Makes You Think We Want You Here?"]
p. 245
Barnum Bailey "Greatest Show on Earth" circus poster, 1908.
Billy Rose Theatre Division, The New York Public
Library. New York Public Library Digital Collections,
http://digitalcollections.nypl.org/items/510d47da
-4ed7-a3d9-e040-e00a18064a99.